R A P T U R E

RAPTURE

SUSAN MINOT

Alfred A. Knopf   New York   2002

The author would like to thank her beloved editors, Ben Sonnenberg and Jordan Pavlin, and early readers Amy Hempel, Nancy Lemann, the Minots Carrie, George and Eliza, Lucy Winton and Tripp Lewton for their orienting feedback; and Charlie Pingree, for standing by.

This is for HF Moody III, earliest supporter.

THIS IS A BORZOI BOOK
PUBLISHED BY ALFRED A. KNOPF

www.aaknopf.com

Knopf, Borzoi Books, and the colophon are registered trademarks of Random House, Inc.

Library of Congress Cataloging-in-Publication Data
Minot, Susan.
Rapture / Susan Minot.—1st ed.
p.   cm.
ISBN 0-375-41327-8
I. Title.
PS3563.I4755 R37 2002
813'.54—dc21
2001038377

Manufactured in the United States of America
First Edition

RAPTURE

HE LAY BACK like the ambushed dead, arms flung down at his sides, legs splayed out and feet sticking up, naked. He lay in the familiar bed against the familiar pillows he'd not seen in over a year. Eyes closed, face slack, he might indeed have been dead save for the figure also naked embracing his lower body and swiveling her head in a sensual way.

◆

HE OPENED his eyes, barely, and looked down at her. He looked with cool, lowered lids at her mouth pressed around him. As he watched he felt the pleasant sensation, but it was not making it up to his head. The good feeling remained relegated to what was going on down there. It stopped in the vicinity of his hips. He did like it, though. Who wouldn't? He especially liked seeing her down there after this long time.

He had no idea what had gotten her there.

He certainly wasn't going to ask her about it. There was no way he was going to wade into those dangerous waters and try to find out why she'd changed her mind or what she was thinking or why she'd let him back in or even *if* she'd changed her mind. He didn't want to jinx it, their being in bed together. Besides, he didn't really want to know. If he'd learned only a few things in their long association—and he considered over three years to be pretty long—one of them was that when Kay did tell him what was going on in her mind, the report was usually not very good. *I honestly think you don't have any conception of what love is.* She had a knack for being blunt in a way he didn't particularly want to deal with at the moment. He preferred this side of her, her solicitous side, which he was getting the benefit of right now.

And even if he did want to know, he no longer trusted himself to ask her in the right way or have the right response ready for what she might say. He'd learned that, for them, there *was* no right thing to say. Plus, he didn't want to risk the subject of Vanessa coming up. He couldn't face that. Whenever Vanessa's name came up, it always ended badly. Of course, it worked the other way around, when Vanessa brought up the subject of Kay Bailey. If Kay Bailey came up things were likely to take a turn for the worse. He might be dense about some things, but he'd learned that.

But wait, now that he thought about it, and being in this position allowed his mind sort of to drift and wander, Kay had already brought up the subject of Vanessa—earlier while she was making them lunch. She had her back to him, standing at the counter. She did not pause from slicing tomatoes in long, patient strokes when she half turned her face back to him. 'How's Ms. Crane?' she said. A little alarm alerted him to check her face and he saw no clenched jaw which he interpreted as an encouraging sign and so told her that he and

Vanessa were still talking, which was true, and that Vanessa had not *ruled out* the possibility that they get back together, which was somewhat stretching the truth. It was, instead, a reflection of what he *hoped* the truth might be, despite the fact that Vanessa had told him *in no uncertain terms*—that was the phrase she used—that it was finally and absolutely over and she could not imagine them ever repairing the damage he'd done. Except that she did happen to be saying this sitting on the edge of the bed where they'd just spent the night together. So all was not lost. She was still *seeing* him. He didn't bother getting into these specifics with Kay. He wanted to be honest, but no one wants complete honesty if it's going to rip open your heart.

Kay had simply nodded, uncharacteristically not reacting, and put the lopsided bread in the toaster. She was in one of her calm frames of mind. At one point while they were eating she looked at him in a pointed way and smiled, beaming.

'What are you smiling at?' he said, a little frightened.

'It's good to see you,' she said. She looked genuinely happy. He did not understand women.

Like a draft in the room he could still feel how bad things had gotten and didn't expect to see her beaming at him this way. He certainly hadn't expected ever to be back in here either, in her small bedroom with the tall window and the afternoon light going along the long yellow curtain. He looked up at the ceiling. It told him nothing. But he kept his gaze there. If he was going to make sense of this it would be easier if he didn't look at her or at what she was doing to him. Instead, he thought, he should just bask in the sensation and, if he was lucky, it would take over his mind.

✦

GOD, he was lovely. God, he was sweet. God. God. God. This had to be the sweetest thing she'd ever felt, nothing had ever been sweeter. It was overwhelming, the feeling that this was pretty much the only thing that mattered, this being with him, this sweetness, this . . . communing . . . this . . . there was no good word for it.

Her fingers encircled the base of his penis and she ran her parted lips up and down him, introducing her tongue like a third lip. Her other hand traveled over his stomach, exploring. It stopped. It moved over his hips. Her palm rested lightly on his skin, as if she were testing the heat over an electric burner. The palm descended, flat. It was a wonderful feeling: skin. Her brushing back and forth was hypnotic and lulled her. With her head bowed she glanced to the side with blurred lazy vision and saw his arm lying there on the sheet. The veins were raised over the back of his hand. She liked seeing his hand there, the manliness of it, and liked the fact that it was his hand and certain, and love for his hand spread through her. It seemed so large for how narrow the forearm was. She closed her eyes and brushed over him, not hurrying. His hand was certain while he had always been uncertain. But this, she thought, this. It . . . was . . . really . . .

✦

BUT HE COULDN'T empty his mind. He hadn't seen her in so long. He'd finally gotten used to not seeing her. When last had he? Once eight months ago. Probably not two or three times in the six months before that. Her refusal to see him had been part of the continual attempt to enforce *something*. Not that she wasn't right to, not that he didn't deserve to be barred and not that it wasn't the best thing for her and, truth be told, for him. He had himself told her she was better off without him. He himself had admitted he was a sorry bastard and that she ought to have run away in the opposite direction the moment she saw him. He was the first person to own up to that. Not that he actually thought she'd believe him. It's easy not to believe the bad things about a person when you first meet, particularly if you're kissing that person. But he had warned her. He couldn't be accused of trying to put one over on her, or of pretending to be something he wasn't. He'd let enough people down recently not to be maintaining certain illusions about himself.

Still, he wasn't going to take the blame for everything. Not everything was his fault. Some things a person can't help. Was it a person's fault if he fell in love with someone else? Could he have stopped that? He couldn't've helped it. How does a person *help* falling in love?

Or, if you were going to take first things first, how does a person help falling *out* of love? That was the problem before anything. He'd fallen out of love with Vanessa. He still *loved* her, he'd always *love* her, but he wasn't *in love* anymore. He'd just lost it. So was it not understandable if a person found it difficult to face the excruciating fact that the person he'd fallen out of love with happened to be his fiancée?

Well, he did face it. He hung in there. And, given his reasoning, he didn't think it so outlandish to believe that if he just stuck with her anyway she hopefully wouldn't notice that he, the guy who used to plead with her to marry him, to the point that it became a running joke, no longer felt the same lovestruck urgency. After all, they had been together for eleven years, which made the lack of urgency not surprising, but also in a way kind of worse.

So anyway you do your best. You continue with the plan to get married—fortunately no date has been set—figuring she'll never notice the difference and will be spared the hurt. And it might haunt you a little, but you figure deep down that this is what was bound to happen over time anyway and that one can't stay in love like that forever. So you are pretty resolved with the situation when into your preproduction office of the movie you've been trying to make for the last eight years, which is finally, actually, coming together, walks a production designer named Kay Bailey who has a way of frowning at you and looking down when you speak as if she's hearing something extra in your voice. And slowly but surely is revealed to you your miserable situation in all its miserable perspective.

◆

THE BEDSPREAD was sloughing off the end of the bed, the white sheets were flat as paper. This is not what she'd pictured when she asked him over for lunch today. It really wasn't. She may have changed her shirt a couple of times dressing this morning and put on lipstick, then wiped it off. It was Benjamin, after all. But she was not planning on winding up in bed. She was well aware there'd been other times in the past when she'd met him ostensibly as a friend and it had been known to evolve that some admission like *I think about you still* or the more direct *I still want you* would cause a sort of toppling of their reserve and before she knew it she'd find herself blurrily pushing him away at the same time that she was kissing him. When she finally managed to separate she would be half buttoned and unbuckled and the internal army which she'd had at attention to face him seemed to have collapsed into a dreamy, entwined heap. And, she had to admit, there'd been times when things had evolved a little further. She wasn't perfect. But there definitely were plenty of times when she *had* remained polite and restrained, when they didn't talk about matters of the heart or, to be honest, about anything important to either of them. That's how it'd been recently, for over a year now. Or more, if she thought about it. It always helped to resist him if she were sexually in thrall with someone else. Then the troops would stay at attention, no problem.

But now, at this stage of things, she'd thought as she set out their lunch plates on the Indian bedspread which covered her plywood table, enough time had passed that she could feel safe whether there was another man or not. (At the moment, there was not.) Isn't that what everyone said? That after *enough time had passed* you wouldn't be affected anymore?

What did they know? Look at her now. With him. Time hadn't protected her at all. Fact is, time had thrown her in the opposite direction. Look where it threw her: back in bed with the guy. And with fewer qualms about being with him than she'd ever had. Apparently time eroded misgivings, too. No one had mentioned that. No one mentioned how time saturated relations between people with more meaning, not less.

None of this undressing would have happened *without* the passage of time.

It wasn't exactly adding up as she'd figured.

Small tentative blips of danger appeared on her radar screen, but they were easy to ignore. The little alarms of the mind are less likely to be detected when the body is taken over by pleasure.

✦

THE FIRST TIME he met her he was struck by something right away. She was leaning in the doorway of his office, a head with a fur-fronted hat like the Russians wear, talking to his assistant. He hardly saw her, a figure out of the corner of his eye, but that was enough. His chest felt a thump. When she walked in, he looked away. Not that she was so amazing-looking or anything, but there was something *promising* about her. His body felt it before he even knew what it was. Somehow his body knew she was going to change things.

She was wearing a blue Chinese jacket with all these ties on it, and when she sat down at the table she undid some of them but didn't take off the coat. She sat and listened to him like a youth recruit listening to her revolutionary assignment. She even knew something about Central American politics. He gave her the usual spiel about the script, which of course she had read or she wouldn't have been there applying for the job, but he had to rely on automatic because he was feeling strangely backed into himself. He felt as if most of what he was saying was ridiculous, but it didn't really bother him because he was also feeling strangely vibrant. She stayed very still listening to him, frowning, businesslike which was in contrast to the flaps on her hat, which were flipped up kookily and trembled slightly when she moved. She kept her mouth pursed in concentration. Every now and then a twitch escaped from her mouth, as if it wanted to say something but was restraining itself. He told her about his struggles to get the movie made and cracked some usual jokes. He made her laugh. That was one thing he knew how to do, make a girl laugh. Her laugh had relief and surprise in it. It had a lot of girl in it. He wanted to keep making her laugh.

She asked him, 'What was the first thing that made you want to make this movie?' Her brow was furrowed. Her mouth twitched as if suppressing a smile. It was a normal, regular question, but it seemed as if no one had ever asked him it before, or, at least, not with the interest she had, and he felt as if she'd just inserted one of those microscopic needles into his spine to make an exploratory tap down into the deepest recesses of his psyche.

It was weird. He liked it.

He hired her. On her way out she surprised him by sort of lunging toward him as if she was about to fall over. She grabbed his arm and gave it a squeeze, not in a flirtatious way—he had made sure to mention Vanessa, the fiancée, all that—but it somehow hit him *more* than if it had been flirtatious. It was full of goodwill, and strong.

That night walking home he wondered about her, telling himself he was wondering about her the way anyone wonders about someone he's just met and is about to work with. He wondered about where she lived and what her life was like and if she was involved with anyone and what she was like in bed, just normal idle thoughts.

He saw her again a few days later at Liesl's loft, where they'd agreed to meet before an art opening. Liesl was a pot friend he'd met during his brief employment moving works of art, and she'd suggested her friend Kay for his movie. Kay was there already and opened the door to him and led him back into the gigantic room. As he followed her he could see her shape better. She was wearing jeans and a small sweater and giant boots. She had narrow hips without much of a waist, but with a sloping curve at her lower back. A strong urge to get near that body expressed itself in his becoming mute and planting himself by a window, a place he'd spent many hours, since there were no chairs in Liesl's loft. Kay and Liesl were crossing back and forth in the narrow door across the room, still getting dressed. What were they doing? They looked ready to him. During one of his times of estrangement from Vanessa a few years before, he'd found himself back there in Liesl's bed. Just that one time. Liesl had been his *friend* for a reason; she wasn't his type. She looked too—how would he put it?—exhausted. You heard people say that whenever men and women were friends they secretly wanted to sleep with each other. But he never wanted to again. Just that once. Watching them arranging themselves in the mirror above Liesl's paint-encrusted sink, he felt intuitively about this new woman Kay that she probably shared a lot of the same interests that he had. At least, more than Vanessa. Though he loved Vanessa. He told himself that. It was like a refrain, one he often returned to since he'd fallen out of love with her. It was his concession to fidelity to remind himself of his continual love for Vanessa in the presence of this new woman.

Later at the opening he glimpsed Kay across the crowded white room. There were people in bulky coats and a muffled din. He felt a sudden proprietary feeling when he saw her gaze up at a tall guy with a goatee. What was that guy saying to her to make her eyes shine that way?

◆

SHE SANK INTO the familiarity of him and let the mainline of sex do its work. Benjamin was like that, a drug. He was the *lure of the abyss.* She drank him in. He was like a strong liqueur trickling down, so warm inside you, you wonder, Have I been so cold until now?

Yes. It was starting again, the humming of the blood. She let it carry her. What was that Oscar Wilde quote?—how the advantage of the emotions is that they lead us astray. The humming spread through her. She felt how wound up she'd been. What relief this was. She was tired of having to look out for herself, tired of beating through thick brush. She didn't realize how tired. Trying to sort out the right way to behave if she was going to get where she wanted ultimately. Which likely wasn't this. At least, that's what she'd convinced herself of. The whirring in her ears seemed to indicate tanks receding, called off to fight other battles.

For a moment the rushing stopped like an engine switched off and her languorous feeling was suspended. She was momentarily stranded, staring at the soft bulging veins an inch from her face. It often happened at some point during sex: the oddness of what she was doing, in this case, swallowing a man's private parts, pumping him up and down. He wasn't making a sound or a movement. For an instant she felt the absurdity of sex like a wink from a wise man standing in the corner.

Then she saw herself and him as two soldiers, survivors on a battlefield, too exhausted even to moan, united by the fact that they'd both gone through the barrage and both were miraculously still breathing.

The thing to do was to press on. The sensation would come back again. Sometimes you had to help it with the right attitude.

So, pressing forward, she continued rhythmically tending to him, lips firm. An image appeared of an oil rig on a dusty Texan flatland. She let it fade. It became pistons in a factory assembly line. Neither was helping her to press on. She steered her attention out of the factory and into an alley behind a bar where a door was open to music playing and in the shadows were a man and a woman. The man's back was against a wall and he was pulling up the woman's short skirt. He told her to get down on her knees. The woman did what she was told. She was wearing high boots. She unbuckled his belt and unzipped his pants and began doing the same thing Kay was doing. Kay sort of merged with the woman. The ground was hard under her knees and the man's hands were guiding her neck, binding her. She went over other details of what was going on in the alley, someone spying through the door, the man lifting her shirt to feel the woman's breasts. Dwelling on this scenario intensified the less varied activity of what Kay was actually doing there, ministering to a silent Benjamin.

◆

ONE MINUTE he was watching Kay's shiny eyes in a mob of people and six weeks later he was knocking on the ocher door of that modern run-down hotel in Mexico City in the middle of the night, having called from two floors above, waking her, to ask if he could come down and talk to her. The next day was their first day of shooting and he was nervous, he told her. He couldn't sleep. Would she mind if they went over a few things? He still had some worries. All of which was true, but also true which he *didn't* say was the fact that he couldn't stay away from her. Some dogged animal instinct was propelling him those two flights down to her in her room.

When she opened the door he could see she'd been asleep. She squinted at him sideways. 'I'm glad you have no qualms about letting me know how I can be of service,' she said, which didn't necessarily mean defeat, but it wasn't what you would call a shoo-in. She was wearing a long-sleeved Indian thing reaching to her knees which would have been see-through if the thin fabric had actually hit her body anyplace, but it fell around her, loose, white, fitting only at her shoulders.

He looked at her shoulders now, with nothing on them. They were the same, so why did he feel so different? A woman's body always looked different before you got it into bed. Sometimes when he'd gotten too used to a body, like Vanessa's, he would trick himself into imagining that he was conquering it for the first time. But it was hard to conjure that up with Kay now. All his conquering in the past had just resulted in a lot of misery. He'd sort of lost his appetite, at the moment, for conquering.

✦

SHE WASN'T in love with him at the beginning, that didn't happen till she was well into it. She wasn't a complete idiot. She wouldn't have let him into her hotel room that night in Mexico if she thought he was someone she might fall in love with. They were working together.

She let him in that first night because there was no way she would fall in love with the guy. Besides he had a fiancée back in New York. That made it safe. Nothing would come of it.

So she let him in that first night. Later she wondered, was that her first mistake? No, she decided. One way or another they would've ended up here, here in her bedroom in New York on an afternoon in June, having traveled more than three years from that couch in the room of a Mexican hotel.

She had let him in. It was no one's doing but her own.

He went straight for the minibar and extracted little bottles of rum and whiskey and mixed them with Pepsi and sat cozily beside her, joking about his worries for filming the next day. He made her laugh. He was not unflirtatious. She didn't stop him. She was trying, at that particular junction, to do some forgetting of her own.

He made her laugh. That was the main point. Though later she wondered whether anyone would have made her laugh. She was sort of ripe for it.

It had been late when he knocked and now it got later. She told him she was exhausted and needed to sleep. He ignored her and kept talking. She was tired, but she liked his talking.

For the third time she said, 'Really, I've got to go to bed.'

He flopped forward into her lap. 'Can I come?'

'You are insane,' she said, but she was laughing.

'Come on,' he said. 'Let me stay. I'll keep very still and lie very quietly beside you.'

They were both laughing. Laughing made everything harmless and carefree and sweet. That's the sort of idiot she was, taken in by an easy laugh. Laughter took the danger out of it. It was one way to get a woman: make her laugh. It disarms her and distracts her from the perils that may, and most likely do, lie ahead. Laughing throws a person's balance off, and in that state she is more easily toppled.

Why not laugh with this guy? she thought. Maybe her recent bad luck was the result of being too serious. The animal trainer she'd met when he brought in the lions for that car commercial had said she was too rigid. (This was a man who hadn't wanted *any major thing*.) Maybe here was a time to loosen up. If she continued to steer herself too stiffly, she'd never grow or expand. One shouldn't try *always* to be certain and sharp and right. It probably did a person good to go slightly against her principles. A person could maybe learn something. Maybe in certain situations it could do *both* people good. And how would she know till she tried? This was her chance to branch out. Though this rather drunk, boyish, groping man might not look on the surface to offer her expansion, Kay saw there was, tucked inside him, a call to adventure.

But she was still on the fence.

Then he pulled a guerrilla tactic. Into the joking and the laughter he introduced a serious tone.

'The first time I saw you I knew my life was going to be different.'

She held the smile on her face, waiting for the punch line. She would have rolled her eyes at him if he'd looked at her, but his head was bent forward.

'I know that sounds like a line and you're probably thinking, Who is this asshole?'

Her smile sagged. He was sounding different and his face was changed. His face was not looking happy.

'And I thought, I don't know what I'm going to do about this. Because I already have someone in my life.'

Kay had the ghost of a smile.

He looked down into the can of Pepsi between his hands. 'The only reason I'm saying this is because I'm drunk.' He shook his head. 'I couldn't stop thinking about you. Isn't that ridiculous? And want to know something even more ridiculous?' He looked at Kay, angry, as if this were her fault. She had stopped smiling now. She was doing her best to make her face placid and not reveal the strange physical effect his words were having on her. 'I kept thinking about you and I thought to myself, If she asked me to throw everything away for her, I'd do it.'

Kay got the same disconcerting feeling one has listening to the ravings of some lunatic on a street corner when, in the midst of the screaming, one hears a profound truth.

Despite her appreciation for loosening up, Kay had not, since the moment she'd first let him in the door, since the first moment she met him for that matter, abandoned the deep and hidden skepticism which underlay all her relations with men. That part of her remained as alert as a watchman, quick to spot strange movements and to anticipate possible strategies. Of course, the fact that she was giving him so much attention should have been the first indication that she was letting her guard down.

She had learned that when you believe everything a man tells you, you are lining yourself up for a direct hit of disappointment and heartbreak, so it was best not to believe certain grand pronouncements. But she was human. And there was still an unjaded place in her thirty-four-year-old self that allowed for the slight tiny possibility that what he was saying might turn out to be real and that this might, in fact, be big. You never knew when the big thing might happen. It might happen anytime. (That it *would* happen was a given. You never heard anyone say, 'You know what? In some lives the big thing just never happens. Some lives simply miss it.' No, the big thing was like death, it happened to everyone.)

Somehow she relocated herself to the bed—she had an overwhelming urge to lie down—and somehow he had followed her. She was under the sheet and a flimsy blanket. She allowed him to lie on top, but she kept the sheet taut over her chest, barring him. He managed to nudge himself under the bedspread. They were laughing again. They were chummy, cozy.

Then he did something. He proprietarily wrapped his arms around her and drew her close to him. He did it in a way that was nonchalant and robust. She was shocked how nice it felt. She was always surprised how good a person felt. It was shocking. It was one of those rare instances when reality outstripped imagination. Up to that point in their acquaintance he'd been very much a foreign entity, a person making her laugh, a person she did not, in any great degree, fathom—i.e., what was he doing in her bed at four o'clock in the morning, with a fiancée back in New York? No, he was not understood. But once he put his arm around her, he became inexplicably familiar. She'd had a preview of this feeling that night at the opening with Liesl when she stood next to him in the crowded elevator. She felt something radiating from him. For a fleeting moment she had the strange sensation that she was standing next to herself.

You couldn't be sure which way it would go, the first time you touched someone. Either the person would be familiar and the way he held you would sort of take your breath away, or he would remain a stranger and though your breathing would be affected, the way he held you would be odd and unknown, like arriving in a foreign country and being hit with its smells, which are intoxicating but about which you remain uncertain. It was not the all-consuming feeling which comes when you arrive at a place you've known well, after being away a long time, so that some things are changed, giving you a new thrill, and since you see it with new eyes, it is both old *and* new, both familiar and strange. That is always more powerful. Benjamin was like that to her. Familiar and strange. But powerful things usually contain complications and with complications come trouble, trouble of the sort that certain people spend their whole lives avoiding, or, if they were like Kay and most of the human race, looking for.

His arms were around her and she felt stilled, like a glass of water. Did a man feel that, too, the slow melting of the self? Did a man get the same orders? Not likely. A man had a different drive.

Even now, here in her bedroom where the light had spread into a glow across the wall, lighting up the room indirectly so it was like being in a yellow tent, even now she could remember that first night and how the dawn showed up glass-blue by the black wilting palm trees and was cut into long strips by the dangling metal blinds.

His putting his arm around her had been the real start. That was the bolting from the quiet house, the setting off on a sudden journey. That was the physical decision which got made on its own.

There was no subtle prod toward love. People would never get together without some kind of hydraulic urging. Without strong physical insistence, would people ever dare?

She could remember that first night in Mexico vividly, the way one always remembers a first night or a first impression or a first kiss. He was trying to pull back the covers in the gray darkness, trying to get in. Now they were laughing again. After the serious moment, it was a game again. She remembered his insistence; she felt it was proof of something. He kept asking her questions—*Where are you from? What is it like there? What is it like to walk around and be you?*—without waiting for answers. She kept laughing. He kept tugging. He made it under the blanket. She asked him, 'What are you doing here with a fiancée somewhere else?' He didn't laugh at that. He sort of flopped back and stared at the ceiling (much like he was doing now, she thought, at least as far as she could see out of the corner of her eye with her head bent like this, though she couldn't tell if his eyes were open or not. That night they were open, staring up, worried.) 'I don't know, Kay,' he said. The room was suddenly quiet with only the air conditioner humming. 'I'm here to find out.' He looked at her. She felt dread. She felt a thrill.

He pulled the last cover back with an impatient sweep and settled in beside her. His face was stern. He reached down and encountered fabric and pushed it aside and encountered more and pushed that away and finally got through and touched her. He rose up on one elbow to look at her. He had an amused, revelatory expression, as if to say, I have been given the impression all night that you have wanted to keep me out and now I am finding evidence quite to the contrary. It was hard to forget the expression on that face.

◆

AT LEAST they'd *had* Mexico, he thought. At least, that.

But he could not recall the enchantments of Mexico without being reminded of the night of her desertion, near the end of the shoot when he'd stayed in the hotel to wait for Vanessa's call. Back in New York Vanessa was entertaining one of her artists, a guy from San Francisco who seemed to Benjamin to be gay but about whom Vanessa made a point of relating that he was always hitting on her. Kay knew why he was staying in the hotel and went defiantly off to a club with some of the crew. When the group returned very late, bursting into the lobby and streaming into the bar where Benjamin waited over his vodka, Kay was not with them. Neither was Johnny. Johnny, his DP, for chrissakes, the man shooting his movie, the person other than Kay closest to him in these last two months. Kay and Johnny were notably absent. The next morning Kay left early for Miami, as planned, having gotten a commercial for a couple of days which meant money, something Benjamin couldn't offer, and he hadn't seen her before she left and had to endure the cracks on the set that day about Kay and Johnny disappearing from the theme brothel they'd gone to after the disco, not knowing, or at least pretending they didn't know, what had been going on between Kay and himself. He felt sick all day.

He finally reached her on the phone in Miami and confronted her. She didn't admit or deny anything, but flabbergasted him by saying she hadn't thought he expected exclusivity. Her voice was cool and he wondered with panic if this was the woman he'd allowed himself to fall in love with. Just the other night they'd stayed in that thatched place in the jungle, and under that pink mosquito net he'd felt that he'd very possibly found the woman of his life. She was good and reasonable and skeptical and true and whenever he rolled over and looked at her another surge of love, or lust at least, would sweep through him and he'd reach for her again and each time she was drawn easily and willingly into his arms.

'What about the other night?' he screamed. He was losing his voice, he was a wreck. 'Weren't you exclusively mine the other night?'

'Would that have been the night,' she said, 'you were waiting for a certain phone call?'

He hated when they weren't direct. If she were just direct and came out and said what she meant, then he would be able to respond to her, but this half-insinuating, half-accusatory . . . it bugged him. 'I'm talking about three days ago,' he said. 'In that pink bed.'

'Right.' It was a whisper.

'What about that? What about then?'

'That was lovely.' She sounded uncertain.

'I thought you were mine then,' he said.

'I was.' She was barely audible. She was far away. In Miami. Who was she, anyway? Did he even know her?

There was a long silence. Then she said, 'But I'm not the only one, am I?'

The thing was that during those last few weeks in Mexico he had seriously been thinking about leaving Vanessa and seriously been trying to figure out how he could do it. But that had been when he was certain of Kay. Now he wasn't so sure. And with his uncertainty came the end of the short period of happiness they'd had, and the beginning of the misery.

✦

GOD, men were nice.

He was nice. When she thought of all the time she'd spent agonizing over him and thinking about him and fighting the idea of thinking about him and dreading him, she felt how truly sweet it was to accept him now with an open heart. She thought, This is what it must feel like to be a saint. Full-hearted and ecstatic. Though no saint she could imagine would have been in precisely the same position she was in at the moment.

✦

THEN HE GOT back from Mexico and watched Kay withdraw. He had loosened his grip for a moment after the Johnny incident and she stepped back. And why wouldn't she, really? He wasn't *offering* her anything. At least, not yet. He needed to figure things out. But he still wanted to see her while he was doing that. He could only offer her the fact that he loved her, which he did and which he told her whenever he managed to convince her to see him. But by then her reaction to him had changed. She wasn't listening to him anymore with the same attention she'd once had, looking like someone with earphones on, watching his face at the same time she was listening for confirmation from somewhere else, from a voice in those earphones.

No, after they were back in New York in their old lives, by then she was sort of scoffing at him. One time standing awkwardly in her small kitchen when she was impatient to have him go—she explained with very female logic that it was because she wanted him to stay—he told her he *wished he could be with her* and her response came through her nose in a little snort. She wasn't buying it anymore. She had started to buy it, she told him, for a while, in Mexico. But it was different back in New York. Nothing had changed in his life. He tried to explain it to her: things were complicated. She nodded. She regarded him with a blank expression which was worse than scorn. He could see how maybe it didn't *look* as if he loved her, but his hands were tied. What could he do? He had other people to consider. Another person, that is. He'd been in this thing too long a time to *just walk away*. He owed that person too much. He really did.

Kay didn't argue with him. She just listened, arms folded, standing against the stove. Her expression said, You're full of shit. But she was still listening and as long as she was listening he was going to keep talking. He needed her to understand: Vanessa had saved him. He didn't put it that way to Kay, but

tried to *convey* how Vanessa had stood by him all those years
while he was struggling to get the damn movie made. Truth
be told, she'd supported him for a solid year in there. Then
on and off for a few more. How did you repay someone for
that? At least now he was pulling his own weight. (Though it
did help that he didn't have to pay rent. Vanessa's owning the
apartment was a definite plus. He saw it as a matter of good
luck, for the both of them. She had the good fortune to have
family money and it was no skin off her back and they both
benefited. She was starting actually to make money with her
gallery and that money he considered distinctly different
from the family money. The money she earned, he'd never
take that money. She worked hard, and even if it was her family money which she'd used to back the gallery in the first
place, she was now earning it herself. A lot of girls wouldn't
have bothered working at all. He admired Vanessa for that.
But he wasn't going to pretend that he didn't *like* the fact that
she had money. A woman with money was less helpless. A
woman with money could choose. She had power. So, because
Vanessa did happen to have money, she ended up, he admitted it, taking up a lot of financial slack. But a lot of it was
out of his control. She was the one who wanted to be by the
sea in the summer, so *she* took the share on the North Fork.
He would have been perfectly content to slump his way
through the summer in town stringing together visits to air-
conditioned movie theaters, but if they were going to *spend
time together,* then he had to go out there and when he did there
was bound to be the inevitable mortifying moment when he
didn't have enough money to chip in for the tuna or the
booze or whatever it was they were all madly consuming in

that disorganized house. What else could he do? He was broke.)

But it wasn't just the money that made him indebted to Vanessa. Everyone made too much of money, he thought. (He dimly acknowledged the fact that this assertion was usually made by those with not much of it.) The more important thing, though, with him and Vanessa was what went on emotionally. She had supported him in much more important ways. She encouraged him through those long deserted stretches when if he had to go out one more night and answer questions about what he did and have to say again *working on an independent feature* when he'd rather have put a bullet through his head. She'd stuck by him when even *he* didn't think he was worth sticking by. And it wasn't as if he didn't love her for it. He did. She was . . . well, his best friend, he guessed. They'd been together since college nearly the whole time. With only a few on-and-off periods. Part of senior year was one. And after graduation when he *needed to be on his own*. He moved to Paris. He'd gotten a scholarship. The idea was to study film, but he dropped out of the school and used the money to watch two or three movies a day (easy to do in Paris), which he thought was as good a way as any of studying film, actually, but extremely lonely. He thought a lot about Vanessa, but was not ready to . . . to . . . what? To be only with her.

So he had little flirtations in Paris, mostly with other Americans at first. Then he branched out to the more adventurous Swedish hippie and eventually landed an actual Parisienne (though she was technically from Dijon). Vanessa came to see him once and they fought the whole time. They had agreed *to be honest with each other* about the other people they saw, despite the fact that it never made either of them feel better. But neither of them would admit to wounded feelings and instead tossed back and forth little grenades of amorous details—the length of hair of a girl he'd messed around with, the skiing weekend she ended up in bed with two guys but *only kissed one of them*. In telling the stories they'd begin tentatively, concerned with each other's feelings, then, as the stings increased, would find it not so bad after all to divulge more. He remembered one fight (but not what it was about) walking by the Seine on some gray afternoon and how she stormed off and he waited for a few good hours before finding her again in the café near his apartment (belonging to friends of her parents). She stood out, a big-boned blonde, clearly American, at the corner table with a cup of coffee, scribbling furiously in a little book. When he approached, she reached for her cup and drained it, not looking at him. When she did look up, red-eyed, he saw she wasn't mad anymore. 'You had the keys,' she said, suppressing a smile of relief. 'So I had to wait.'

By the time he moved back to New York they were both so emotionally worn out from the separation they fell back on their original arrangement of being only with each other. Since Vanessa already had an apartment—she was in her short-lived art school period—it was only natural he'd moved in. They never really discussed it. He stayed with her when he got back and just kept on staying. After six months they were engaged. He couldn't remember the actual moment they decided. There hadn't really been one. He hadn't gotten her a ring or anything, it just became obvious. It wasn't really official. Though she definitely wanted to, Vanessa didn't want to tell her parents yet, not until Benjamin's career was a little more established. He agreed with that. His career wasn't exactly what one would call *on solid footing*. So they kept it between themselves. Though her family did like him, at least her mother did and that's pretty much all you could expect as far as the family was concerned. Her father was too much of a Washington bigwig to notice his daughter, or any of his children for that matter, having weightier problems to occupy him. His wife catered to him despite his pretty much ignoring her, which was his general attitude to everyone not in a powerful position. Though at one Thanksgiving Benjamin did feel a beam of curiosity pass over him, only to be followed by Mr. Crane's temporary registration of suspicion.

So in all the time they'd known each other he and Vanessa had always been somehow in each other's lives. In a way, she already was his wife.

And it wasn't as if he didn't love her anymore. He incessantly repeated this fact to himself because frankly he was appalled at how these other feelings could have developed. He'd fallen in love with someone else and suddenly *she* was crucial to him. *Her* body was what he needed. He couldn't help it. What he could help was not leaving Vanessa. So he didn't. After Mexico, he stayed. He stayed despite the fact that he grew more and more depressed. He thought obsessively of the one he was in love with, the one who wouldn't see him, who wasn't even going to *consider* him until he moved out. He'd wake in the morning lying next to Vanessa and think of Kay first thing and make love to Vanessa before she had to get up for work and while she was in the shower he'd think of Kay again and of the time they stayed on the beach till it got dark late and how she had that purple thing wrapped around her chest and how the whites of her eyes looked and how they had to climb back over some wall and the way she stepped around the green glass shards sticking up in the cement along the top like shark fins, moving as if she were a tightrope artist. The thought came to him then very naturally and without hysteria that he could see having a child with her. He had not had that thought before. Not with Vanessa. Then he remembered being under the mosquito net in that pink bed in Oaxaca and how soon after that she'd gone off with Johnny. Hearing the apartment door close behind Vanessa and the bolt click, he'd ask himself, lying there in Vanessa's bed, if he was really in love with this other person who no longer was giving him the joyous feeling he'd gotten at first in that country far away, who instead was sinking him into a quagmire of suffering and agony. The answer bled out in front of him as an unfixable blot of doom, the same answer each time: yes.

The sun had moved into the room so it was brighter. He preferred rooms dark. He looked down at Kay, as if to remind himself where he was, and thought there was a time he would have been dying for this.

◆

IT WAS HARD to believe she was here with him again, naked. What had happened to that last ironclad resolve, supported by the other ironclad resolves before it, not to see him again, or more importantly, at least never to touch him?

She'd not seen it coming. Then suddenly there he was, touching her.

They had finished their sandwiches. The water was heating for tea. He came up behind her at the sink washing dishes and put his arms around her. It was a friendly clasp, one he might have given her in the past, affectionate, not as an overture, but holding on tight and firmly as if to keep her from floating up. At first she felt it in that friendly way. Then the pressure of his arms and their insistence made her feel more. *You matter to me.* She had felt that insistence before and knew that it was possible for it to take her off down a road at first wonderfully lush and appealing which very quickly deteriorated into an impenetrable mass of brambles. But not being angry at him anymore, she wasn't looking to him to soothe her. She had let that go. She felt his breath on her neck. An unnerving susceptibility moved through her. His breath on her skin. That was not false, that was . . . she felt unsteady. Small disturbances went off inside her. She put the plate down in the sink with the water running over it and stood unmoving, holding her breath like a person staying still so as not to be detected by an intruder. He was slumped against her, his head dropped fecklessly on her shoulder. She stood paralyzed, feeling his lips resting on but not kissing her neck. She had no thoughts, but felt as if she were barreling toward a revelation.

She was aware that she was responding, in part, to the effect of touch. Touch had a particularly compelling quality when it came from a person who'd been away for a long time. But it was more than that. This physical reminder was conjuring up remnants of their whole history together. The familiar smell of his hair and skin dusted off an array of feelings and thoughts—the uneasy exhilaration, the longing, the shocks, the scorn usually followed by understanding. In encountering these phantom feelings again she found her eye could pass over pretty much all of them, but stopped staring at one: his body against hers.

This bodily fact purported to be the truth.

The moment was split for an instant by the future. It was always an unnerving sight, the future. It was uncertain. But during revelatory moments like this, the future asked for quick consideration to test her orientation. Would this revelation take her where she hoped to go?

Eventually, at some point, Kay figured, probably, she would, most likely, have children and that a man would, in all probability, be a part of it (which was not necessarily a given these days). She had always allowed herself a certain fuzziness on the subject of her ultimate future. She didn't see herself walking down the well-trod path of domesticity. She sort of sidewise conjured up a semidomestic arrangement tilting away from the *totally* conventional one she'd experienced with her parents. She hadn't exactly worked out the details. Her vision was a little spotty. The persistent but dim notion of *finding someone* had blotches around it of suspicion. What she had observed of family life and lasting love seemed to support the despairing conclusion. She looked for models, but what she saw was either unsuitable to her temperament—she couldn't imagine catering to *that* husband—or unattainable— she wouldn't know how to keep that more desirable one happy.

She had not, however, given up hope that she would work it out when the time came.

Every now and then that hope would solidify into a certainty. It would happen while she was watching a movie and the hero or heroine would make a decision—usually to *choose love* or, at least, to leave a life of habit behind. Those were the moments she wanted to be living all the time, decisive moments, moments when she was doing life justice. Now as she stood there pressed against the kitchen sink with a man hanging around her with a kind of desperation, she realized that this *was* one of those moments. A bulletlike thing shot through her long-held refusal to consider Benjamin Young and she was hit with the distinct possibility that Benjamin Young, wayward and indeterminate as he was, might very well turn out to be the person destined for her.

But wait. The past was speaking: she had left this guy over and over. What was the difference now? She had it; he was no longer attached. He was not living with Vanessa. He was living alone. Her body did know something after all. Benjamin was free. It was a start. In truth, it was the start she'd asked him for at the beginning. She had the feeling she'd walked into a house she thought she knew well and discovered a room she hadn't seen before. Maybe it wasn't too late. Maybe they did have a chance. She was overcome with the same fateful feeling she'd had the night of the art opening when she stood next to him in the elevator, that there was something of herself which had suddenly leaped over, into him, and was now located inside his body.

She reached for the faucet and turned off the water. Without leaving his arms, she took his hand and led him past the stove, switching off the burner with a flick, down the hall and back to where he'd not been for some time into her bedroom.

◆

HE LOOKED AT her bare back with the vertebrae pressing through the skin below her neck and at her shoulder blades like the base of wings. He was always surprised by how small her bones felt when he touched her. She looked the same; her hair was shorter. He liked it better long, but it looked all right short.

The strongest impression he'd gotten when he'd first walked into her apartment was how much it smelled the same, like woodsmoke and a sort of flower smell, he didn't know what it was, but for a moment he didn't just remember the emotions he used to have there, for a moment he actually felt them. Her apartment still had amorphous shapes of piles of things covered with fabric and tucked in the corners. It was how Kay stored her shit, the opposite of Vanessa, who was always throwing things out. Vanessa kept her surfaces clean and liked her edges sharp and colors this side of gray or beige. It was funny how different they were, Kay and Vanessa, but also the same. They were both willful and both had a softness which came out in sex. But where Kay whispered, Vanessa cooed baby talk. Where Vanessa stamped her foot and shouted when she was angry, Kay clenched her jaw and became stonily silent.

The women had met once, before Mexico, on the stairs of the production office. Benjamin was walking Vanessa out because she liked to be looked after and put into cabs, and as they came down, Kay was coming up. He introduced them, feeling strangely excited, and they both gave each other big smiles. *Oh great to meet you,* they said, and *Finally.* Vanessa towered over Kay. Even one step down, she was taller. They both waved good-bye warmly and Benjamin thought it had gone well till he opened the taxi door for Vanessa to get in and she said, 'You want to fuck her,' before ducking into the backseat. He laughed at her, a sort of choke-laugh, and told her she was being ridiculous. It was the same thing he was still telling her to this day. *You're being ridiculous.*

Wasn't that right? Why cause the woman more pain than he already had? Vanessa had a pretty good idea *something went on,* but at this point in time would it really do any good for her to know exactly what? Not as far as he could see. There was rarely any good in telling. In fact, he had pretty much adopted it as a general policy to never, if you could help it, admit anything. It had never helped, in his experience, to admit anything. You just got punished for it. His male friends all corroborated this: never tell. That is, except for Jeffrey and Andre, who believed in full disclosure. But they were gay, which explained their different perspective. He could not remember a time it would have made things better to tell— his few experiments (O.K., when he was caught) led him to precisely the opposite conclusion: to tell made things decidedly worse.

Anyway, aside from his time with Kay in Mexico, what was there to tell Vanessa? Most of it went on in his head anyway. Vanessa didn't need to know that Kay refused to see him. Or that the few times she did see him—well, Vanessa would have blown that way out of proportion. From the start Vanessa had a little radar thing about Kay, which was, at that point, based on nothing. Just imagine if he'd given Vanessa even a little something to go on. She would have run with it. Women always blew these things way out of proportion.

✦

SHE SHIFTED up on one elbow and resettled around him. She tended to him with reverence. The more she lavished attention on him, the more her self seemed to fade. That's what she wanted, selflessness. She wanted to forget that self which lay awake at night full of dread, wondering, *What is going to become of me?*

When she was a kid she used to lie on her lawn staring up at the herring gulls riding the airwaves. She wished with all her little being to be a bird, off the ground, swooping.

So much of the world didn't add up. So much of it was a disaster area. And so much of that had to do with being earthbound and made of flesh. That she was able to transcend the world through that very flesh—to find relief as she did now in sex—was one of the many paradoxes in life. It was little twists like that, when the problem could also be the solution, which made her almost believe in God.

It was one thing to touch a person for the first time. It was one of the headier things in life. But to touch a person one has known, after a long time has passed, that was even headier. And if that person was never actually yours to begin with, then the combination was overpowering.

What a relief it was. She felt anonymous. She imagined herself doing the job of a whore. This was a whore's job, after all. The more degraded she felt, the more saturated with sex, and happier. Her personality was dissolving into a sex personality, there to be used by him however he wanted. She was not particularly feeling his manly strength at the moment, he was not even moving, but she was aware of it in him. It was in him somewhere, that driving urge to overpower her. She'd felt it before. And there was some evidence of it here. As an animal might, she was finding the evidence with her mouth.

She ran her fingers lower on him. She flicked him softly.

She felt as if she were climbing soft steps, building on the last sensation. A hot wind seemed to blow through her, expanding her volume but not her weight.

Was this going to take her where she hoped to go? Well, for the moment it was definitely putting her where she wanted to be: out of herself. And it wasn't complete obliteration since she was turning herself over to another person. She liked to think of it as devotion. It even felt religious. Though it wasn't exactly the devotional sort of selflessness they were talking about in Sunday school.

Her thoughts drifted to the other times they'd been together like this. Those scenes were fixed there, unchanging. The time he steered her over broken glass in that seedy bathroom in Oaxaca with the turquoise floor, the time with the heart carving over the bed and the couple shouting through the wall. She liked thinking of the time she started to unzip her dress and he stopped her. *No leave it on.*

Then there was the time, it was many times, of her with crossed arms, telling him to go away. These images were less distinct, overlapping. Then another image of them standing outside her building, breaths showing. She was slouching against him. And the conversations on the phone, the hours eaten as she stared at the things in front of her on her desk, her jar of colored pencils, her piles of clippings, the snapshot of her sister, the alabaster snail, the red jackknife, the eagle feather, hearing his voice but stuck with these things and wanting to be where he was and enduring long silences and telling him to go away. God, it was sweeter now to be feeling instead, Take me. She flung herself into it. It was like throwing herself onto a bonfire.

◆

AFTER THEY got back from Mexico, he couldn't help calling her. 'Why are you calling me?' she'd say, and he would answer with the only lame answer he had: he was in love with her. He wanted to see her. You want to see a person when you're in love with them. Since she wasn't letting him see her, he said, at least she could let him hear her voice. That's all he wanted, just to hear her voice. This explanation would be met with silence on the other end of the line.

He hadn't figured out exactly what it was he did want from her, or how he *could* fit her into his life. He was merely expressing the immediate fact that he couldn't bear not to have her in it.

One phone call stood out in his recollection, probably one of the last before a long stretch of no contact—that was their history: long stretches of no contact—when Kay lost it. She burst into tears. It was not what he'd come to expect from Kay; Kay was self-possessed. He'd watched her remain implacable on the set once after an actor threw a fit, picking up an overturned table while the rest of the crew watched with glittering eyes. It was more like Vanessa to cry. Vanessa expressed herself. She wept and yelled at him. She hurled videocassettes, which flew like hockey pucks across the polished floor.

Those were the worst days, sneaking out to buy cigarettes so he could call Kay from a phone booth. It was a bad movie. Rainy nights, getting drenched, around the corner from the apartment so he wouldn't be spotted. There was a phone booth in a nearby pub and he called her with bad music playing in the background. Her voice, which had once been velvety and low, turned hard and unforgiving. I have a friend over, she said curtly. He kept trying. At least she was still listening. One time her voice was soft again. She listened to him say he was dying for her. He was. But there was nothing to add to that. They listened to each other waiting.

Then one time she told him to leave her alone. He felt it like a whip across his cheek. It didn't stop him calling. She started hanging up.

He called only rarely then. He didn't call as much as he wanted to. He made an attempt to restrain himself. It was agony. He often called after he'd had a few drinks when it was easy to drop one's resolve. That was one of the beautiful things about drinking: it inspired one to drop resolves.

After a few hang-ups, which, let's face it, are hard to take, he tried writing her letters. He wrote a couple, but it wasn't so satisfying. He found he didn't so much want to let her know things as he wanted her *response* to them. So he started sending her faxes. He struck a lighthearted tone. He was good at that. At first she answered lightheartedly back. He was encouraged. And with encouragement came a lapse back to his desperation. Her response to that came rolling down through the plastic slot on a piece of paper: WHAT DO YOU WANT FROM ME? He answered back in very small handwriting that he just didn't want to lose her.

But hearing Kay weeping shocked him. 'Please please leave me alone,' she said. She sounded as if she really meant it. She sounded like a little kid.

He seemed to be surrounded by weeping women. That was when he was editing the movie, when watching the footage would bring back the very texture of the days in Mexico, the stale bread at breakfast and the slatted chairs on the terrace and a black dress Kay wore and the shape of her calf and tears would spring into *his* eyes. It was ridiculous. Everyone was crying. And, really, what was so bad about their lives? They were all pretty damn fortunate, if you looked at it on paper. The whole thing was pretty fucking pathetic.

Through barely open eyes he looked at the yellow tulip Kay had in a bottle on her thickly painted white bureau. He noticed a footprint on the wall a couple of feet from the edge of the mattress. It was hard not to think of the months he'd dreamed about being here in her bed with her doing to him what she was doing now. He touched her hair, affectionately, limply. Things had simply never lined up for them, that was the truth of it.

✦

IT HAD BEEN a year since there'd been any actual sex between them. In the meantime, she'd had sex with someone else, which definitely put a dividing line down. During the brief periods of sex with someone else Kay was able to forget about Benjamin Young. She had someone else to be in thrall with. Mark the gaffer had a lot of physical ardor, though he wasn't much of a talker. Kay thought his shyness was a reflection of a cautious heart, which meant that he was sincere, which after Benjamin Young was a welcome thing, till after three weeks of sleeping together, Mark suddenly went cold. Familiarity didn't warm him up. Just the opposite. Mark turned out to be one of those guys who'd gotten so used to living alone he couldn't adjust to having a person around. One night after making love he retreated to the other side of the bed and explained that he couldn't sleep if he was touching someone. This hadn't been a problem for the previous three weeks which she pointed out and he said he was aware of that and actually that had surprised him, too. This, needing to be apart, was how he really was. Kay didn't take it too hard since she'd always felt like a sort of impostor with him, though it didn't prevent her from taking great comfort in the way he wrapped himself around her.

Now that she was beside Benjamin again, it was hard to believe she'd been with anyone in between. But then it was pretty much impossible to think of how it was having sex with someone other than the person you were with. You could *think* of another person, but as long as your senses were occupied like this, you couldn't really recall the details of another person, or really conjure up that other sex. It was like trying to remember an obscure melody with a marching band blasting in front of you.

She had to laugh at herself, though. A week ago when she ran into Benjamin she'd felt so unsusceptible. It had been a year since she'd touched him—a *relatively* long time. She'd run into him at a screening—that was how he got here. They had both come alone, to one of those converted buildings over by the river, so they sat together. She found with enormous relief that she was able to sit beside him and to watch the movie and to reflect on the fact that the man who had spent so much time occupying her mind was now sitting unthreateningly next to her, perfectly normal, wearing a sort of army jacket speckled with rain, not causing her distress.

The movie was one which left the audience feeling hopeful about life and it further buoyed her spirits. They walked out together, agreeing about the movie (which they usually did), about how the main guy was great but the woman miscast. They chatted like old friends.

'So you've been good?' he said.

'I have, yah.'

'Good. That's good. Me, too. I've been pretty good.'

'Good,' she said.

'A little crazy maybe. But good.'

'Crazy's good.'

'Can be. Unless it's too crazy.'

'That's true.'

It was friendly and normal. She felt as if she were coming out of the other side of a tunnel with him. It was like the last scene in a movie when the two lovers meet again and show a tenderness for each other, despite all the hell they've been through, or in this case, the hell that their relationship was, and humanly accept each other's imperfections and let bygones be bygones. He smiled at her with a full beaming smile, and instead of loathing him for it, as she certainly had in the past, she felt perhaps for the first time with Benjamin a grateful wave of goodwill toward him, an emotion untainted by lust or anger.

They walked a few blocks together, stopping and starting—they both had other dinners to go to—and nothing could have been more natural as they shuffled along smelling the river air and the rain on the tar than for her to suggest that maybe they should get together sometime and have him say yes right away. It reminded her of one of the things she'd always liked about him, that he didn't hesitate, that when she invited him someplace he never said he wasn't sure or that he was too busy or that he'd call her later, but always let her know right then and there if he could make it or not, and if he couldn't make it, would immediately suggest a time he could. Not a few of her friendships in the city had languished, then dissolved for lack of that kind of attention. So she asked him for lunch two days later at her place and he said he'd see her Friday. It had not been the last scene in the movie after all.

After they parted she walked to her dinner with a new-found energy. She felt she'd been given a tank of oxygen. And why shouldn't she feel better? It was a lovely night and she'd salvaged something from a damaging, painful relationship which she'd been sure was lost and beyond hope. And she was not hoping for more than simple friendly relations. She passed by a building where she'd once worked years ago on a low-budget film. It looked bombed out and taped over and she had a momentary impression of walking in a city where there'd been a war and hostilities had recently ceased and the ruins were now peaceful. A soldier might have told her that this could be one of the more dangerous and vulnerable times in war, when things look serene, but before a truce has actually been signed.

◆

IT HAD a life of its own. He didn't need to be thinking of where it was or what was being done to him for it to respond independently. He didn't need to be paying it any mind. In fact, he'd noticed that sometimes when he did think about it, the vibrancy in it would falter and wilt.

He watched Kay. She looked absorbed in a nice, slow way, applying herself. He felt oddly distant. He knew he'd once had a sharp, finely tuned feeling toward her, but he couldn't locate it. Must be all the pollution of the last few months, he thought. Everything was corroded. It was impossible to think in a fresh way. He couldn't imagine ever getting back to anything fresh.

He could remember *about* the sharpness of feeling, even if he couldn't feel it at the moment. He remembered one time at the beginning when they'd met in her hotel room after a half day of shooting and how nervous he was to be with her and excited and full of fear and how he sat on the arm of a chair and pulled her over by the belt. His hands were shaking and he tried to hide it by clasping her around the waist. He pressed his head into her chest. She was wearing a shirt the color of lettuce and a little silver cross. She took off some heavy silver bracelets, clanging them on a glass table, her hands moving with the same efficiency he'd seen when she was arranging tiny Mexican figures in a crèche on the set, decisively, without a pause. She was smaller than the body he was used to. The white afternoon blazed silently outside the blue-trimmed windows and lying beside her he couldn't remember having wanted anything as much as he wanted her. She made so much noise he had to clamp his hand over her mouth. No, it certainly was not like now. That day was like something murky at the bottom of the sea.

He'd never get to that again. Sure, he remembered it. Fuck if he couldn't forget it. It would be better if he could. He would also just as soon forget that morning in the prop room with her in a Mexican dress up on the table, forget how they got no sleep, how in bed if they weren't rolling around they were laughing or talking. What about? A lot. He couldn't remember exactly what. The story of their lives? It seemed more than that, bigger. Whatever it was, he felt ridiculously close to her. But there were the other things that came along with it, which he would happily forget, too—the pit in his stomach, being unable to sleep, the worry. It was terrible being away from Kay and terrible feeling guilty about Vanessa. All those feelings in the past, he couldn't forget them. But he wasn't able, and probably frankly was too ruined, to actually feel them again.

So, now, cut to three years down the line. Him, here, with Kay again, but with his earlier self worn away. He felt snapped off, like a heavy branch creaking on a tree which one night just doesn't make it through the storm.

◆

IT WAS, from the start, perverse. She was aware of that. She was both drawn to him and repelled. She was attracted to the audacity of a man who could one night in a thatched bar tell her he was falling in love with her and the next day on the set be overheard, while she was hanging a crucifix to hide some wires, telling the script girl how much he missed his fiancée back in New York and how much he wished Vanessa were there with him. When Kay heard that, having slipped out of his arms only a few hours before, it repulsed her and, also, God forgive her, made her want to be with him immediately.

It got worse, the longing for him. It still filled her with dread to think of that period. She would fantasize about applying herself to something worthwhile and dutiful, welcoming derelicts into homeless shelters or cradling AIDS babies in preemie wards—anything the opposite of the self-absorption. (Now and then in her youth she had made small forays into public service, but after the initial charge of being part of a march or counting envelopes filled with checks, she grew discouraged by the bureaucratic busywork, the inept organizers, the sitting in windowless rooms. The suspicion grew that what she was doing was distinctly ineffectual, made worse by the expectation that it was supposed to be so affecting. That's where the movies came in. In those windowless rooms she found dramas resolved and complexities explored. People had character and bravery in addition to beautiful faces. Things came together. Things made *sense*. And even if life wasn't like that, it was consoling. It actually helped her live.)

Oh, Christ if she knew. She was tired of thinking. Tired of thinking about Benjamin. Tired of trying *not* to think about Benjamin. She was tired of trying to adjust to what she thought she was *supposed* to do, and of trying to work out whether something was against her better instinct, or if her better instinct ran counter to the better practical thing, only to find out when things didn't work out, which was the only time you seriously analyzed your behavior, that an instinct which had appeared and been rejected turned out to be, at least to some degree, correct. With experience you were supposed to learn when to trust your instincts. For instance, you should not, as people were always advising you, against your instinct, *give the guy a chance* if you really had no interest in him. There'd better be *something* to start with. She'd learned, too, that it was not prudent to tell a new lover, in the early days of getting to know each other, details of your amorous past, as your instinct might be urging you to do in the spirit of trust and full disclosure. The lover is not to be believed when he reassures you that of course he can handle it. It is, he might argue, in the past. Don't believe him. The only things truly *in the past* are things completely forgotten.

It was hard to recognize instincts. They got easily tangled up with desires and fears.

But on this sweet afternoon Kay felt mercifully lifted from those petty concerns. Sex, in the form of love—or love in the form of sex, it was hard to differentiate—had swept her up. This was real, this was the most real thing. (Sex made you think that. It blotted out logic. And thank god. What a relief. How did people do without it? They grew ill, they went mad, that's what happened.)

Still, there were contradictions. That feeling of *the most real thing* was capable of suddenly vanishing. One could very well experience a giant *lack* of connection with the very person to whom moments before you were cosmically connected. In any event, if you'd felt that most real thing with someone, you, especially if you were a woman, were going to have a hard time forgetting about it.

Kay was still trying to figure it out. She was not prepared to give up her reverence for sex. It was too mysterious, too powerful, too magic. A kiss for instance. What was it? Two mouths coming into contact with each other, and yet a kiss had the power to make a person believe that not only was love possible, it was really quite likely, not only was life going to turn out all right, there was a very good chance it would turn out gloriously.

So it had its deceptive side. But sex inspired hope, the water we swim in.

Kay's little bedroom was transformed and a strange silence encased it. She had left her petty self behind, and was given over, mind and body and spirit, to the mystery.

✦

WHY WAS HE remembering all this shit? It was all flooding back to him and it wasn't making him feel any better. But did thinking about the past ever make a person feel better? He doubted it.

He looked at the partially open door leading out to Kay's little hall which led out to her little living room. He remembered one afternoon—it was always the afternoons with Kay—when she must have been feeling all right about him because she'd let him come by and it was snowing and they sat on her couch holding on to each other and watching the snow and hardly talking. He thought of that afternoon often. He could feel that afternoon more than he could feel her here now, sprawled across his hips. Sitting with her that day, he'd felt weightless. The snow was coming down thick and every now and then a spasm of wind sent it spiraling behind the black fire escape bars. They didn't have sex or anything, they were just peaceful. She'd made them tea and he remembered at one point she fished the tea bag out of a cup and squeezed the water, then flicked it into a wastebasket across the room, a fly dunk. Everything was lined up. Her hair was long then. She used to hang it over his face. She'd drag it back and forth over his chest, doing this playful thing, but with an absent sort of stern expression. He thought of kissing her in the cold outside her place on the East Village street with stray people walking by in the dark. Was that the first winter or the second? He couldn't keep it straight, but he remembered the bulky coat around the body which he wanted to get at and only being able to touch the skin on her face and kissing her mouth which was warm and wet in the cold dry air and that her mouth tasted like milk and how her eyes stayed open just beneath the dark fur of her hat.

He knew more bad than good stuff had happened between them, but he blocked the bad details out. He remembered the good details better. One afternoon which he might have remembered as the day he told Kay that he had finally decided, ten months after Mexico, that he was not going to leave Vanessa—it was definite, they were discussing the wedding again—instead he remembered as being one of the days he and Kay ended up in bed. Once it was clear where things stood, going to bed wasn't going to complicate things further. It was a way of saying good-bye. After they got dressed, she was in that lovely mood he hardly ever saw, when her eyes were soft and she laughed lazily and was relaxed in general and wasn't reprimanding him for things he couldn't help. She walked out of the apartment with him and for whatever reason (the sex probably—it usually had a pretty good effect on Kay) she was not morose or blaming. Maybe they'd been through enough of that. It was a nice evening in late September with the streets quiet and the shadows long. It was unusual for them to be out in daylight together. He felt between them an air of resolve and understanding, as if they were an old married couple who knew by now what was important and what lasted and what didn't. They walked for a while together with her holding tight on to his arm till they came to Washington Square Park where the sky was lit up pink behind the church steeple and he felt as if all the people going about their business seemingly unconcerned were actually extras in a movie, having shown up for their benefit. He said good-bye to her and she smiled and kissed him on the mouth. She had her hair in a ponytail and he watched her walk away, the person he loved. The further she got away, the more the extras started to turn into actual indifferent people, college kids with backpacks, people taking little steps walking their dogs, lone men muttering *spliff ludes uppers,* and the pink sky spread above all of them and if he thought about it he could also say that that day might be remembered as the last time he'd felt anything close to being in love.

✦

SHE SORT OF lost respect for him when he wouldn't move out. Not that Kay understood all the complexities of his relationship with Vanessa Crane. She only knew some of the things which had gone on between them. But if he could be believed, which frankly, at this point, she had to admit he probably couldn't, his heart had been telling him to get out of this relationship for a while. But he wasn't listening to his heart. He was, as he said, taking other things into consideration. He called those things obligation and loyalty. To Kay they looked like avoidance and denial.

But Benjamin was not unlike many men. He would rather endure twenty years of misery than face ten minutes of discomfort.

But who was she to say?

She had purposefully not been encouraging about urging him to move out. She wanted him to make the decision himself. She saw him as being perched in one woman's nest and ready, with a signal from her, to fly into another's—her own. She feared the opportunist in him, the way his face would light up when he saw the prospect of a financial backer. Additional unnerving feelings no doubt sprang quite naturally from the singular fact that he was, after all, cheating on his girlfriend.

Then, at a certain point, her mistrust faded. Or, at least, her mistrust became diluted by empathy and something she could *handle*. She told herself things were more complex. This line of reasoning was introduced after she'd fallen in love with him. After she fell in love with him, his ambivalent feeling was a cause for sympathy. Frailties were a part of a person's character. His frailties made her love him more, in a way. Fact is, she could relate to his ambiguous feelings. She understood them. She had those feelings herself.

◆

HE COULDN'T leave her. When it came right down to it, he was simply unable. He tried. One time he really actually did try. He told Vanessa he was moving out. It was a Friday night. How he managed to speak the words still amazed him. They'd been in his head so long he supposed he just had to say them out loud. She wept uncontrollably. He comforted her and reassured her and they ended up talking about a lot of things, things which neither had dared admit before, and afterward felt much better and made up and went to bed. He never so much as packed a sock.

Besides, Kay had never actually asked him to leave. That might have helped, if she had.

What was his choice? On the one hand he had Vanessa, a woman with whom he'd once been in love, standing before him saying she wanted to marry him and be with him for-ever—as soon as a few more things were in place—and on the other hand Kay, a woman with whom he was in love now, *not* standing in front of him and *not* saying anything about the future, only conceding that she might *consider* him if he were free. Who would anyone say was better to bank on?

I mean, here Kay was now, performing fellatio on him when she'd told him a year ago she never wanted to see him again. He didn't get it. He couldn't piece it together.

So he thought of his grandmother's driveway. That's what popped into his head. The way it looked in the fall with orange leaves on the bright green grass. He thought of the model of a ship in her dining room. The *Flying Cloud*. It was always in the same place on the sideboard for as long as he could remember. But someone else lived in the house now, his grandmother was dead and the *Flying Cloud* must've been sold at the auction. At least, he never saw it again.

He looked down at Kay, thinking of the *Flying Cloud*, of his grandmother's dining room which she'd never seen, never would. Vanessa had been there, though.

Kay and Vanessa ran into each other another time, after the time on the office steps. He and Vanessa were coming out of a movie and there was Kay like an electric shock, in line for the next show. She said she was waiting to meet someone. It was during a separation period from Kay and he didn't trust himself to speak. He felt Vanessa watching him. Luckily the girls did the talking, about the movie mainly. Vanessa started to mention something about the plot, but stopped herself.

'Oh wait,' she said to Kay. 'I don't want to spoil it for you.'

'That's O.K. That never bothers me knowing,' Kay said. Both of them being so nice.

Benjamin felt his face sort of puffed up with air and he got the dizzying sensation that he was a balloon hovering beside two of his selves in the form of these two women. He well knew that both of them had said not particularly warm things about the other, privately to him. Would that come out now? He was aware, too, that these women had the capacity to compare notes which would result in the uncovering of he could only begin to imagine how many lies.

'Have a good movie then.'

'I will. Nice to see you.'

After they walked away, Vanessa turned to him with slow, blinking eyes.

'What?' he said.

'That was interesting.'

'What?' He pretended he didn't have a clue. So often he really didn't have a clue, he figured this could easily be one of those times now.

'Your crush,' Vanessa said.

'Sweetheart,' he said, as if this were a chuckle between them.

Vanessa arched her eyebrows, a sign of the loss of her sense of humor. 'I can tell by the way you were acting,' she said, staying cool.

He told her, as was his habit, that she was ridiculous. He couldn't remember how the rest of the night went, but chances were: not so good.

He'd gone back and forth between them in his mind: Vanessa was his family, his comfort, something he could count on. And Kay, she was more like himself, but like a new self who wasn't such a failure, who had made a movie. Kay was a new vista. Sometimes you got that feeling when you met someone—the horizon widened. Most of the time, after you got to know the person, the widening feeling went away. You got used to the person's vista. But with Kay the feeling had lasted. In his better moments he could believe that with her, he might become the person he wanted to be. Then he would review all that would have to change and it would look impossible.

Anyway, all the weighing of considerations turned out to be beside the point. When it came down to the moment of truth, he simply couldn't leave Vanessa. So the decision got made by default. What it meant, though, was that he would have to forget Kay. Which he started to do. He applied himself to the project. But it took longer than he would have liked. It took too long.

✦

SHE GLANCED UP in the direction of his chest and shoulders, which was awkward with the position of her neck, and she saw him with his eyelids hooded, just barely looking down at what she was doing. Or was he looking past her? There he was, as close as could be, beside her and under her and even in her, and she hadn't the faintest idea what was going on in his mind.

Somehow she didn't want to know. Not if it wasn't good. And knowing Benjamin it could easily be not good. She hoped, at least, that he was in the same general arena of transport as she was. There were no guarantees, but she was doing her best in that department.

She zeroed all her attention in on him. Surely he must feel how she was worshiping him. It was a paradox that the more she focused on what she was doing the more she disappeared. Her mind drifted in a still way . . . if she thought too much about *his* thoughts she'd lose that drifting. Any practical thought that appeared was like a raised nail on a smooth wooden floor. Following a dreamy train of thought kept her in a voluptuous haze. She pictured him chasing her through a burnt, ravaged landscape and catching her and throwing her roughly down on a hill of dirt and pinning down her arms and brutally taking her. That was a nice thought. She stayed with that.

◆

A PLANE FLEW overhead, low, out the window. You didn't notice planes much in the city. When he was little, planes were so rare he and his brothers used to run outside on the lawn and point up when an airplane went by.

After he made the decision to stay with Vanessa, bleak months followed. The only time he wasn't miserable was when he saw how grateful she was. She dropped her chin and gave him her maternal, cherishing look and he was proud he'd stuck with her. People gave you a lot of credit for that, sticking together. They admired it. Apparently, sticking together was good, in and of itself. No matter what might be going on inside. So Benjamin hung on to that notion. At times it even seemed true.

He convinced himself he'd done the right thing. He certainly didn't believe in abandoning a person who'd been good to you. A lot of women wouldn't have put up with his unemployment, or helped so much with the movie, or thrown that party, or put him in touch with the guy who knew the guy who helped get him into the San Sebastián film festival which, even though it wasn't big, was a good one, and got him his foreign distribution. And even though *The Last Journalist* didn't have an American distributor yet, it did have its own little impact. After he screened it in Washington, the U.S. embassy in Guatemala had set up an investigation into the disappearance of Amy Anderson and the Red Cross workers with her that day. Of course, it had helped that Vanessa's mother knew the ambassador and helped arrange the screening. Still. So once things were happening for him he wasn't going to be one of those assholes who abandons the person who'd been there all along, in order to take up a new life with someone else.

Though sometimes he wished he were one of those assholes. He had once pictured himself married to Kay, and liked how he saw himself, hardworking, with Kay carrying their kid in one of those chest straps. But here, in this moment, he saw himself with Kay objectively, with her bare arms draped over him and the somewhat unnatural position of her face being sort of passively assaulted by him and he got the unnerving feeling that he was, in fact, another kind of asshole. Of what kind exactly, he couldn't say.

+

SHE COULD FEEL the cleft on top with her tongue and the raised contour of the veins against her lips if she kept them soft.

Sometimes it put her off, doing this. Contrary to what she assumed she was supposed to feel, she did not always find the penis to be an object of fascination. When she was young, it had been foreboding. It had taken her years of familiarity to develop a fondness for it. For a long time it was out-and-out frightening. But like sex it had many aspects to it.

When she first became lovers with a man, it was the private thing she felt too shy to look at. She couldn't say why. Because there were other times when she didn't feel shy, when the man was familiar and easy and she very naturally held it warmly in her hand and felt how sturdy it was and how this was privately him and she'd feel protective and think how important a part of him this was, to him, and therefore to her, and how despite its sturdiness how it was also vulnerable. She liked how, by simply holding it, she could feel it grow, like a plant, slowly filling her palm, becoming bigger than it seemed it was going to. Then it would lose its vulnerability and become aggressive, weaponlike, something she very much wanted plunged into her. But it could also be something athletic, full of vigor, boyish. In a different mood, she saw it transformed again, into a kind of totem at the center of a ritual, almost sacred, with the power to bewitch.

It was curious, taking one form in repose, then quite transformed when activated. This activation, Kay had been told, was not necessarily even registered in a man's mind. She'd heard a man describe the surprise of looking down and seeing himself protruding. A man could become aroused and apparently not know it. It was like a separate creature. A woman did not have that. A woman's excitement traveled through her mind just as much as to the other parts of her body. While her temples were pounding, her wits were aware of it. On some level, the body knows that a woman is the one who carries the consequences of this excitement. A woman definitely knew if something was happening. She became it.

Kay took Benjamin in slowly, keeping her teeth back from the ridge of the soft helmet. If she took him in too far it'd make her gag. She'd learned to do a sort of flexed thing with her throat. She bumped him gently back there.

◆

SO—TYPICAL—just as he's finally adjusting to his decision to stay with Vanessa, just as he's finally making peace with it, Vanessa decides she's had enough.

She hits him with it on a Sunday night, a time when no people should ever try to talk about anything serious. She sat on the couch lighting one cigarette after another. 'Is something bothering you?' he said. Actually, she said, there was. He'd changed. She no longer felt appreciated by him. He was no longer there, he was absent.

Come on, he told her. It was the movie. He'd been busy with the movie and the editing had taken longer and with him finally working she wasn't getting the attention from him she was used to getting and she— No, she said. It wasn't that. It was more than that.

She was right, of course, but how did she know? How do women know these things? He didn't even know it himself till he could look back on it and see she'd been right.

To top it all off, he was just starting to feel as if he were falling back in love with her. O.K., maybe it started when she said she wanted to split up, but the fact remained the same. That night in bed he held her tenderly and felt how precious the body in his arms was to him. He realized how deeply he loved her. He always had. He forgot that he'd stayed with her because he hadn't wanted to hurt her and saw now that it was because of his real true and abiding love—it just needed the threat of her leaving him to reveal itself to him.

He begged her for another chance. She didn't dismiss him completely. He paid extra attention—meeting her at work, enduring a dinner with some of her clients—but it didn't pay off. It was too late, she told him. She was fed up. She asked him to move out.

For a long time it'd been what he'd wished for, that Vanessa'd kick him out and he could go to Kay without feeling responsible and guilty. But now that she was doing it, he was consumed by jealousy. He was sure she'd met someone else. He finally got it out of her: No, there wasn't someone else yet, but there might be. Women had a way of putting these things. *Might be.* There definitely *was.*

He found a sublet in a basement full of some guy's knick-knacks which he thought would be temporary but was where he still was now, a year and a half later. Kay saw it once and asked him how he could stand having all this other person's shit around and he said he didn't mind it. That was one thing which had unnerved him about Kay, she wasn't particularly tolerant when it came to other people's shit. Chances were she probably wouldn't've put up very well with his. Vanessa, however, had. Pretty much. While he and Vanessa were together, she had.

All of which further pointed to the necessity of getting Vanessa back. Vanessa had accepted him totally. If she wouldn't take him now, who ever would? He needed to prove to Vanessa that he had been worth sticking with this whole time.

✦

SHE WASN'T in love with him at the beginning. It had been a safe feeling when she wasn't in love with him. The safe feeling disappeared when he began to be necessary to her. What had happened to change him from a safe, unloved person into the dangerous, pain-inducing one she was in love with? As far as she could trace it, it happened one afternoon.

It was the afternoon she heard Dave Jacobs had died.

Dave was someone she knew from around town, a photographer who was always returning from some war-torn country or about to leave for another. He had a wide circle of friends, and was the sort of completely irresponsible guy who's expected for dinner but doesn't show because he's probably run off with someone's wife after which he'll make best friends with the husband, one of those guys irresistible to women despite a total disregard for personal hygiene. Years ago Kay had spent a long night dancing with him and whenever she saw him afterward had the feeling she'd been to bed with him, which she hadn't, but Dave Jacobs left her with that feeling.

Jane Warburg had been the one to tell her. Jane was one of those people who seem to know everyone, yet are oddly lacking in personality. Kay was irritated to answer the phone and hear Jane Warburg's droning voice. 'Am I bothering you?' It was a typical Jane Warburg opening. Yes, she wanted to say, but instead acted as if she was busy. 'Did you hear about Dave Jacobs?' No, said Kay, irritated Jane Warburg had gossip about someone for whom she had proprietary feelings. 'He's been killed,' said Jane.

Kay felt the air retreat around her. She had a strange, wooden awareness of her hand holding the receiver. Dave Jacobs had been in Costa Rica, there was a bus accident, the bus slid off a mountain road, everyone was killed. Apparently some chickens survived, Jane said. It was odd the things people said around death.

When Kay got off the phone her heart was pounding in an irregular way. The apartment seemed relit, or tilted. At the corner of the table the tablecloth dropped with a weirdly angelic fold.

All the colliding thoughts she'd had moments before of whom she had to call and what bills she had to pay immediately lost their importance and she saw how transparent they'd been all along and how death was far more pertinent. She saw how within its pertinence there was also absurdity, the absurdity that this man who talked to dogs on the street and who grabbed girls solemnly by the hand to lead them away was no longer anywhere on the planet. He was simply gone. She felt a sob rising in her.

Then the phone rang. It was Benjamin. He was in the neighborhood.

It was during a *not supposed to be calling her* phase. During this ban she was trying not to expect anything. Only very tinily secretly did she. He was engaged, this guy. So things had been intense in Mexico. It was easy for things to be intense in Mexico. They were making a movie, they were in the bubble.

It was easy to feel joined with someone you didn't know very well if you were near him every day, working through the night in a jungle in a small area lit by lights, if you drove for miles on bad roads so there were hours for talk inside an enclosed space. And it was not hard to be in thrall with someone you'd just started sleeping with because when that went well, the thrall pretty much automatically increased, for a while at least. And with that joined feeling it would be easy to blithely accept that your time together was limited and that when you returned to your lives, you would return apart, and that it was possible to take what was good between you and to prize that and have no regrets. It was easy to believe all that in the jungle.

Back in New York, she was embarrassed by the direction her feelings had taken. She still had a small creeping desire for that joined feeling to continue.

When he called, she listened at first. She told herself she was being tolerant. When her feelings began to revive she told herself she'd better kill them. She said his name as if it were a hard nut and told him to leave her alone.

But the afternoon Benjamin called, Kay was not the least concerned with managing her feelings. Her little drama with Benjamin Young looked like a toy house compared to the cathedral of Dave Jacobs' death. Kay told Benjamin the news she'd just heard. Benjamin said, Could he come over? Why not? Kay thought. She didn't need to protect herself. On the contrary, she had that dulled feeling which comes in the wake of loss which made her feel: What more can one lose? Matters of fidelity and possession were small compared to the broader ones of friendship and admiration, some of the feelings she'd had for Dave Jacobs.

When she opened the door to Benjamin, seeing him didn't penetrate her in the stark way it usually did. She was numb. He put his arms around her; she stood limp. He led her to the one armchair in the corner (found on the sidewalk years before) and sat her on his lap. Resting her head against his chest, she listened to the vibrations through his shirt as he talked about some *project* he wanted to do and why he was doing it and the money blah blah blah and the experience etc. etc. etc. while in her throat she felt a nervy, hyped-up flutter.

When she started to cry he stopped talking. He stroked her head and the stroking was soothing and good. She turned her face up to him and his mouth was there, close, and when she kissed him it seemed as if his mouth was the perfect and probably only relief there was for this lost feeling of swirling in fog.

They didn't leave the armchair. Afterward when she pulled her skirt back down, she looked at his face and saw something new: she was in love with it.

He had to go. (He always had to go. In fact, Kay figured, even now, years later, on this Friday afternoon as she tended to him, he probably had to go.) But that afternoon, in the first moments of being in love with him, his having to go was all right, because he could never *really* go now, not after what had happened. Anything he did was all right. Now she was on his side. She was in love with him. She had truly believed then that everything would be O.K.

She had genuinely actually believed it.

What had made her fall in love with him then? Kissing him while thinking of someone she'd liked who'd died? Because he got inside at that lost moment? Didn't it have anything to do with his personality? Maybe that he'd made her laugh? Was it because she suddenly felt his gaze reach to the back of her skull?

For a short period after falling in love with him it was wonderful. She felt she was living straight from her soul. She was no longer alone. After a while though it turned, as certain types of love have a tendency to do, into a sickness, and she longed for the time before she'd ever laid eyes on him.

◆

HE KEPT his eyes closed. He felt as if he were whirling down a drain.

◆

SHE PAUSED TO take a breath, knowing that pauses interrupted the building of momentum, but her cheeks were being pulled in a way they were never pulled at any other time. They were a little strained. She didn't want to hurry. That could make it unpleasant. She rested her cheek against his thigh, flushed. Outside she heard the moan of air conditioner kicking on in the building across the back garden, if that's what you could call the lot full of weeds and warped pieces of plywood and bent lawn chairs. The vent let out high-pitched creaks. It sounded to her like a waterwheel creaking in a running river.

After she fell in love with him there was a brief attempt to see each other *on a friendly basis*. There was no poetry in the phrase *on a friendly basis*. He'd kiss her hello with dry, tight lips and hitch his chair away from her at the small marble table of the coffee place where they met. She was used to being close to him and had liked that. That was *how* she liked him: close. She was irritated how easily he seemed to be adjusting. He said he was just happy to see her. But then, he wasn't on his own. He had another person. He always had that other person.

She took him into her mouth again, keeping ahold of him with a hand, fingers encircling his base, rooting him down.

✦

NOT ONLY did he need to prove to Vanessa that he had been worth sticking with, but he needed to address the panic that this would, unless he put a stop to it, keep on happening. He would keep falling in love with women. He would love one woman for a few years like he had Vanessa till things got a little regular, then another woman like Kay would appear and he'd fall in love with her, and even if he never actually *fell in love* with any woman ever again, he was pretty sure he wouldn't be able to say no to the occasional temptation. He didn't see how he'd be able to help himself. He figured he'd better stop it now and try to stick with one woman. If Vanessa didn't take him back, he was sure he'd never maintain a permanent relationship with a woman. A wife, in fact, a person to grow old with, the thing his parents had. His parents had it effortlessly. Despite what his brother thought—his brother was more cynical about these things—he saw his parents as being still in love. So why couldn't he expect to find that?

'Because you're not your parents,' Kay had said to him once. He'd ended up talking about that sort of thing with Kay, about his ambivalence, more than with Vanessa. When you meet a new person, you sometimes get an urge to explain yourself. He told Kay he wasn't sure he'd ever be able to find something like his parents had, maybe it was outside of his personality. He was not as good as they were. And Kay, who usually argued with fervor when she didn't agree with something, must have grown weary by then, weary of his hopelessness, of their hopelessness. 'You're not that bad, Benjamin,' she said, looking pained, as if this were a harder thing to admit than his being a complete catastrophe.

He glanced down at her now resting against his leg and figured she must be getting tired. He better stop his mind from wandering. He didn't have forever. He better concentrate.

✦

SHE SPENT more time trying to forget him than she ever did actually being with him. Obstacles fed the longing. She grew impatient at work, distracted when she was out with friends. Returning home late at night, she'd think, Has he called? She'd told him not to, but one section of herself still pictured him calling, with a miraculous message which would somehow change everything. She knew that for this to happen *he* would have to change, totally, his whole personality. But it consoled her to imagine him suddenly otherwise than he was.

One night she dreamed of a cheetah pacing silently on a long veranda outside windows where she slept. Suddenly it leapt at her window, crashing through the glass and attacked her, biting her throat. When she told him about the dream, he said, unembarrassed, 'That's me. Cheater, cheat-ah.'

◆

IT WAS NICE, though, no question, seeing Kay again, seeing her naked. The last time they'd had sex was in the dark so he hadn't been able to look at her. They'd kept most of their clothes on anyway, ending up in a contorted position in her hall just inside the door. Fuck that seemed like a long time ago. When was it. After the wedding of Margaret, his costume designer. They hadn't really spoken to each other till the very end of the evening. He hadn't been sure if Kay'd be there or not. She was. And he was there alone. They ended up walking out together and went for a drink. At the bar he told her he'd moved out from living with Vanessa and she didn't ask him anything more because, if she'd asked, he *would've* told her he was back in love with Vanessa. But she didn't ask. She was relaxed and inviting, the way she got after a few drinks, and sitting beside her on the dark ruby banquette he felt the old urges.

They rode silently home in a cab and he took her hand. She didn't respond, but she didn't move it away. She looked as if she was sleepwalking. So he was surprised when they pulled up in front of her building where the tree branch shadows were projected by the streetlights, that building where so much emotion had once been, and she asked him did he want to come up. It took him aback. 'Do you want me to?' he said. She shook her head, not at him but at the question, and got out of the cab, dropping some bills on his lap. He paid the driver and followed her in.

Walking up the stairs, she didn't speak. They stepped inside the apartment and she shut the door but didn't turn on the hall light the way she usually did automatically. She turned around and pushed him back against the door and pressed against him with her face an inch away so he could see the dark shape where her eyes were, but not the eyes themselves. They stood with their mouths an inch from each other with her champagne breath on him, not moving for about a minute and a half, which is a long time to be standing in the dark that close to someone with your heart pounding. Out the open window a car went by blasting music which they could hear at the other end of the apartment and she finally moved the inch forward and mashed her lips against his and murmured something which he thought was, I love you so, then thought that maybe it was, I love this song, because the car was still down there waiting for the light to change, but he didn't want to move his lips to ask. It was that Bob Dylan song "One of Us Must Know."

He didn't understand women. He'd only grown accustomed to expecting certain types of inexplicable behavior. For instance, if you told a woman she looked beautiful it immediately cheered her up, no matter how much she was ragging on you or how pissed off she might be. Tell her she was beautiful and it genuinely seemed to make her feel better. Or, he'd observed, women spent long periods of time exchanging obscure information with each other which, if you listened to what they were saying, you could not figure out the important part.

But he didn't need to understand Kay in that dark hallway to like being with her as much as ever and to feel excited when he lifted her sweater and felt the skin on the small of her back and she sank heavily against him.

He looked down at Kay now, and in that coincidental way of two people separately occupied happening to glance at one another in the same moment, she looked back at him, her gaze sweeping sideways, eyes at a low burn, hardly registering him there.

He reached down to her face and gave her cheek an affectionate little slap.

◆

IT WAS AMAZING how much things could change between two people. That you could feel a person was your eternal mate one day and three months later bump into him in, say, the flower district and hardly know what to say.

It was months after she'd fallen in love with him and weeks after they'd not been able to see each other *on a friendly basis*, so it was disorienting to see his figure standing there on the sidewalk, purporting to be like anyone else's.

The weather had changed the way it does in the fall, suddenly cold from one hour to the next. She was walking home from an interview, tired and underdressed, carrying too much in her bag. The wind was smacking into people when they hit the corner, thumping their shopping bags like drums, making their hair fly. She spotted him outside a florist's pointing to a bucket of flowers.

He noticed her and smiled; he was slow, staring.

He gestured toward the flowers. 'For a show in Vanessa's gallery,' he said, and named the artist, as if Kay would be interested. He seemed proud to be doing this errand for his girlfriend. Why was he staring at her that way, straight on?

None of her self was there as they smiled. They nodded. They pointed in different directions. She left with his *Great to see you* ringing in her ears. She walked away, rattled. She felt as if God were watching and testing her—not that she actually believed in God, it was more like a concerned third party—overseeing what was going on between her and Benjamin, watchful of her progress. She didn't know exactly what she was expected *to* do, or what the test was, but instinct told her that walking away from him on her own was the beginning of passing it.

It gave a person a chill thinking about it, how much things could change between people. It only confirmed her impression that the bottom was constantly dropping out of human relations.

So now, here, reunited and joined, that was being on the right track, wasn't it? Wasn't this the state to which all aspired? The forgiving accepting attitude. The dropping of all one's restraint and reservation and mistrust, no longer subject to a back-and-forth, the seizing ahold of something and holding fast to it and giving all to that whether or not you've determined if it was *safe* or promising or even wise. There'd been so many days of saying no to him, then weeks, then months—all those days lay piled in a useless heap. What had they taught her? Anything?

The fact that they were here seemed to render those days worthless. Something had endured and brought them together again. She relaxed into letting go of all that worry.

Things certainly could never be as bad as they'd been. She was sure of that. She felt a strange thing happening: the evaporation of all that old hideousness. This late afternoon of this particular day in June she was getting the distinct, golden feeling that now was their time. Here, in her bedroom with the window open to the feathery trees growing alongside the barbed wire spirals, no one knowing where they were (at least no one knew at that moment where she was), certainly no one knowing what they were doing (*she* hardly knew what they were doing). They had survived something. It was a turning point.

A tiny little pang disturbed her inside. Hadn't she felt this turning point feeling before? Perhaps, said the little dinging pang, perhaps nothing had changed, he was still Benjamin and this was just another version of the same thing. She shook off the thought like a chill and followed the warm expanding feeling instead. She was opening up. That was the better feeling. Maybe something would even come of it. She felt airy hope gathering in her, some impending thing . . . something beautiful waiting over the hill . . .

◆

HE HAD fucked it up. He was well aware that he had done a good job of majorly fucking it up.

◆

SHE WAS full of revelation. In this sultry flexible state she was seeing clearly: all the frustration and sobbing and feeling worthless was the road they needed to travel to get where they were now. That they'd made it to here meant that he was, well, something like her fate. Meant for her after all. The only way to process it was to forgive. Everything. Him. Herself. *That's* what she was feeling, a voluptuous letting go.

She felt strong and direct. She no longer needed to feel like an idiot for enduring the humiliations, for being locked in self-absorption. It was all needed to get her here. It had led to this union. And she could forget it now.

What were once big trees towering over her, the warnings against Benjamin (none of her friends had touted him as a particularly good idea) now looked like wiry needles in the distance. What did other people know about what really went on inside a person? About what a person needed beyond the practicalities? Not that *she* knew precisely what she needed, but she knew what she was drawn to, and those things were not always in her practical best interest. They were the things which made her *feel*. In them was allure and wonder and something which made her marvel at the world, and if there was defiance in them, well, then she'd stick up for it. It made her feel like a scout. Love, as far as she could see, had little to do with reason and practicality, unless you were lucky and happened to be built that way. The choices she made were mysteriously directed and she might as well accept them and not fight them. With her senses hazy from his skin and body, it seemed very likely Benjamin was the ship the gods had sent for her to sail. It was sort of mythical. He may not have been the ship she or anyone else might have envisioned for herself, but that must have been what people meant when they said the person you ended up with was very often *not* the one you would have expected. She seemed to recall that it was usually happy, satisfied people who said that.

✦

IT WAS FUNNY the things that came into your mind during sex. That Lou Reed song with the line *playing football for
the coach.* The street in Providence where he'd gone to college.
He thought of the green where they used to throw Frisbees,
the girls reading on the grass, lying on their stomachs with
their backs bent and long hair spilling down their arms. And
for no reason he could explain, he thought of one night he'd
climbed up the fire escape into a girl's room. He hadn't
thought of that in years. It was before he'd started going out
with Vanessa (though he already had his eye on her, as a lot
of people did. Vanessa stood out on campus—a blonde not
just tall but bigger than other girls, one of those girls *involved*
in college, but who also liked to get high). The time he was
remembering was before Vanessa. He'd gone to a party
where it was dark and narrow and smoky and music was
pounding, where he'd talked to this brown-haired girl he
knew liked him because she'd written him a note after he'd
said something in political science. Her name was Libby. He
hadn't found her that attractive. At the party she was wearing a striped shirt which followed the curves of her breasts
and he still didn't make a pass or anything. He left without
saying good-bye. He prowled around campus with some
guys, and after they'd said good night in that abrupt uncere-
monious way, he found himself, fuzzy with beer, scanning
the windows of her dorm—she lived next to a girl he
knew—and looking up at the beckoning ladder of a fire
escape zigzagging up its side. When he climbed up and

knocked on her window, the girl Libby, much to his amazement, let him in (women never ceased to amaze him) and practically immediately made room for him in her single bed, slipping in alongside him wearing underwear and a T-shirt which he promptly and with her assistance removed. He felt more pleasure in the fact that he'd been let in than in Libby herself, who a few days later left in his mailbox a rather long *note* accusing him of *using her*. She seemed surprised by this, further amazing him. What else did she think he was doing, climbing into her room at 2 a.m.? He hadn't, as far as he could see, from the outset, given her any other impression. This was another amazing thing about women: they didn't seem to want to face some basic facts about men. (Which was probably just as well. They were better off not knowing.) But how deluded do they have to be not to realize that when a boy who never speaks to them and practically doesn't know them knocks on their window in the middle of the night there's pretty much only one thing on his mind and if the girl lets him in, then that's her decision? He's not going to be the one to point out why she shouldn't. He wants to get in! She can be the one to say no. She has a mind of her own.

It wasn't that men and women were completely different in what they wanted, but they were different enough. They had different attitudes. He'd learned some things after thirty years of trial and error. A man had to hide some of those attitudes if he was going to get close to a woman. If a woman knew everything about you, you weren't ever going to make any headway.

✦

MEETING AN OLD lover could be a kind of ambush. You wouldn't know till it happened how out of your system he was. Or wasn't. No matter how grounded you were in the present, your body could send you into the past. Even if all feeling was gone and the person no longer held the tiniest glimmer of fascination, your body could still react and you'd feel it, like the vibration of an old land mine, long forgotten, being tripped and exploding miles away. The jolt got registered in the body. Benjamin gave her that: the jolt. One got the jolt when, in a mild state of mind in an anonymous crowd of people filing into their seats in a movie theater, one recognizes among the other silhouettes one head with its particular brow and particular bristling unbrushed hair bending down to pick something up off the floor as belonging to the body of the person who had once sent wonderful voltage through one's own. Only, now, the voltage received is one of adrenaline and fright.

She'd not seen Benjamin for many months and had moved away from him and the island on which she'd sat stupefied with love for him was now very small and far off in the distance. Enough time had passed that she imagined him vastly changed, so it was a shock when he appeared in front of her with the same translucent skin and the same long hands buttoning his coat and she saw again the shifting of his eyes back and forth on their internal search. His jaw had the same shape. She looked at the area near his ear and saw it as a place she used to kiss. His voice was exactly the same.

A strong jolt alerts one to danger and she got a strong jolt. She was still under his sway. She ought to have removed herself from his presence immediately. But she had not suffered enough. She lingered. She responded to the jolt in another way. He walked her home. They kissed outside in the cold and the drug of him slipped in. She was firm about not letting him come up. It took willpower, but at least that time, she held firm. It hadn't made her feel better. She did the *right* thing and still she felt pain.

◆

HE DIDN'T WANT to think too much about what time it was, but he did have Vanessa waiting for him. Kay didn't need to know about that.

◆

BUT she wasn't firm about not letting him up that other time, months later, after Margaret's wedding. She'd practically dragged him upstairs. Was it the champagne? He did mention he'd moved into his own apartment. Though that apparently didn't make a difference after they lay panting in a dark tangle in the hall: he still left.

He didn't have another woman to get back to, but he still wasn't going to spend the night. He said he was sorry. He made out as if there were all sorts of complications, things he didn't have time to explain. He promised he'd come back the next day and explain them.

He did. He came back the next afternoon. His explanation was the usual. Too much had happened. He was still getting over Vanessa. He wasn't in any shape to be in *any* relationship. He loved her. She must know that by now. But he was too messed up. He just couldn't . . .

As he continued talking, Kay stopped listening. This, she told herself, was the last time she wanted to hear this, to hear a man say he loved her, then enumerate all the reasons he couldn't stay with her and couldn't choose her and point out how actually she was better off without him. She wouldn't listen to this again. She felt hard at the edges and hateful toward him. She looked at the worn spots on her Turkish rug. Doom. Out the window the quiet afternoon moved away as if on a ramp.

He put on his coat and draped around his neck was a new plaid scarf she'd not seen before. Her first instinct was to hug him good-bye, but she stopped herself. She had to stop behaving as if certain things weren't true. They weren't together. They were separating. The air seemed to be draining out of the room. After he left, she knew how it would be: there'd be no air left. Standing beside him she tried to trick herself into imagining they were shouldering this load together, that they were joined somehow, joined in facing their separation, but it was like trying to find oxygen in a vacuum.

◆

HE LOOKED at one of the paintings on Kay's wall, of a greenish sea and two figures about to dive into the waves. When he'd first seen that painting in her bedroom it had seemed so full. Everything to do with her was full. Now the painting looked cracked and unfinished.

Everywhere he looked there was damage. He'd done his fair share of ruining it. He'd lied too much and fucked up too badly and he couldn't change that and basically could never make it up to either of them. Though he was still trying with Vanessa. He hadn't completely given up. Still, there were only so many times you could say you're sorry to someone and be believed and be forgiven and only so many times you could say it and not get sick of it yourself.

◆

HER MOUTH was clamped around him and stretching awkwardly. Odd that this was a pleasure, this odd configuration.

Her first impression of him came back to her. He had not been unappealing. He had a nice smooth face and a sort of shy way of ducking his chin. Certain qualities struck her: he did not press his ideas, which was unusual in a director. He had been unassuming and natural when he stood near her in the elevator that night with Liesl, as if he was accustomed to being close to people. But there were also unnerving qualities. Something about him was not quite intact. She wondered about his sexuality. It seemed sort of blasted. There was an intensity in him, but he didn't seem to know how to manage it. His spirit seemed to be sort of careening. She was surprised to hear he was engaged, involved in such a normal thing.

She used to enumerate those unnerving qualities to herself in an attempt to stop her longing. She focused on his chronic distraction, on how he didn't seem to have a core he might draw on in times of duress, on his ambivalence. After she fell in love with him, however, those things became interesting. They became fascinating human things to ponder.

✦

PEOPLE SAY first love is the strongest. Benjamin hadn't found that. And he'd definitely been in love with Sandy Palmetti in high school in Rhode Island. For years he lay in bed thinking about her, aching. She had a way of biting her lower lip so it sprung out. They used to cling to each other for hours with her sitting on his lap in her cutoff shorts. But his feelings for Kay Bailey had more layers. Knowing more of life made your feelings more dense. Those feelings had survived life's onslaught. The more jaded and protective and disillusioned you became with age, the bigger love would have to be to generate life out of those ruins.

Maybe it was a wonderful thing, falling in love. He'd thought so at times. But that seemed another lifetime. He must've had another mind then. Falling in love with this mind in this lifetime turned out not to be a wonderful thing. It turned out to be a disaster.

✦

THEY SPENT far more time keeping away from each other than they ever did together. She figured it was about a ten-to-one ratio, if that. She could have catalogued each meeting and each good-bye because they were so few and at which ones they'd had sex, which were even fewer.

Meeting in public was the most rare. The night at the Christmas party had been a low point. He stood with her out on a shallow balcony while she smoked a cigarette (she'd started again). The music behind them was pounding and they faced out to hundreds of lit windows and black towers making glowing wedges in the tissuey air. He volunteered that it had gotten easier not seeing her. 'At least I'm more used to it,' he said flatly.

'What happened to it?' she said.

'To what?'

'To that——' she could barely cough out the word, 'love.'

He was drinking vodka and she noticed it made his lips move in a rubbery way. His tone was matter-of-fact as he looked out at the gauzy night. 'I guess it just withered,' he said.

◆

THAT WAS BEAUTIFUL, he thought, the time she stood near him in her dark hallway, standing so close without kissing him. He liked thinking of it.

It was nice, too, that time in Mexico in that bar when he followed her to the bathroom and she sat up on a sink and he undid her shirt and pulled her bra aside. A pink nipple sprung up and he sucked on its softness till it became hard. There was broken glass grinding under his shoes. The vibration of it went up his spine and met his mouth, sucking on her. His arm encircled her tightly and his hand pressed on the curve of her back.

◆

AFTER TWO YEARS, she figured it was safe to go to his office and pick up her drawings from the film. There'd been a long period of separation when she'd not even run into him and she was curious to see him.

Initially it was fine. She purposely did not wear anything special, just her usual black pants, thin sweater. She walked up the steps which had their same tin ring. The office rooms were the same, too, with his secretary Andrea still there, though her hair wasn't navy blue anymore, now it had crimson tips, like something dipped in paint. The desks were in the same place. She did notice a new couch. Benjamin was behind his desk and when he saw her he got up quickly to greet her. He looked thinner and healthy. She remembered right away why she liked him, seeing the planes of his face. Her portfolio was right there leaning on the coffee table, ready to be let go of. She looked at a new picture on the wall. It was by an artist of Vanessa's, a brown and yellow scuttled painting she didn't like, but which she said was nice. He suggested they go out for a cup of coffee and she checked herself internally and found she felt O.K. and was handling it, so they went down.

They sat at the counter of a crowded place where people kept knocking her coat on the floor and he grew distracted with the clattering dishes and orders being shouted and milk being steamed. They talked, as they usually did, about the work he was doing and why he was doing it (still temporary, still just for the money) and about other people they knew and what those other people were doing. Other people were easy to discuss and analyze. He said he'd heard that she was seeing someone and she said she'd just started and he said he was happy for her. Vanessa's name did not come up. Kay didn't ask. Kay knew he was seeing her again—Liesl had told her—though he hadn't moved back in with her. Kay didn't want to fall into the old habit of discussing Vanessa. Near the end of her shallow cup of tea she began to feel a little odd in his presence, sort of shaky, as if she hadn't eaten, and by the time he put her in a cab she felt brittle, like something slowly cracking. Riding home in the cab was like being on an ice floe floating off in a dark sea. She no longer meant anything to anyone. She got out at her building and walked up the stoop with her folder of drawings under her arm and passed invisibly through the small, empty lobby and continued up the stairs to her door. She unlocked the bolts and went robotically inside and walked down the hall to the place in the back where she let things pile up and put the folder down and sat on top of some boxes and started to weep. She wept very hard.

◆

SINCE HE WAS putting all his effort into salvaging this thing with Vanessa, it was easy to put Kay out of his mind. She simply stopped appearing there.

So it was like seeing a ghost when he ran into her at that Christmas party. He'd forgotten how she looked and how it affected him. He had the sensation of a curtain rising, then stopping after a foot. She was wearing a red shirt with small feathers around the neck and beet-red lipstick and he was confused by how real she was and three-dimensional. Her eyes were liquid and glinting. He was feeling particularly wretched about Vanessa so he hardly could register Kay except as someone who carried for him a whole other brand of wretchedness. He'd been going out for a week to holiday parties, drinking constantly. That was probably the beginning of the debauchery, around six months ago. Kay asked him to come outside with her for a cigarette—he hadn't seen her smoke since Mexico—and he leaned wretchedly on the balcony railing, holding his drink. She started talking about what had happened with them and it was like trying to remember a dream which is dim. You know there was a cobbled street or that you were in the woods, but not what you were doing. He couldn't talk about what had happened with them. He didn't want to think about Kay and him. He told her she was out of his mind. He saw her face crumple like paper when he said it, then it hardened. She dropped her cigarette and ground it out. She kept looking down and shook her head. 'You are something,' she said with loathing in her voice. She cocked a shoulder up as if to fend him off. 'Then it wasn't love,' she said, and went back inside to the dark bobbing silhouettes.

He finished his drink out there on his own.

✦

THE DOVE, the one that was always out there, was cooing now out the back window. She felt an affinity to it, to the vibration in her throat. Her lips were pursed in the shape of an O.

Benjamin had not changed and yet to her he seemed changed at this moment. At one time he'd been a man she barely noticed, at another, one she'd cringed from. Now, she was worshiping him.

Life was mysterious. People were always saying that, so why were they always so surprised when they found it was true? Half the time, she was a mystery to herself. Her state of mind fluctuated. Her worldview could just as easily be buoyant and optimistic as convinced that life was blank and meaningless.

Right now, though, her state of mind was dreamy and fluid and sort of roaring. That was sex. But sex could be just as changeable. You never knew the state of mind it might put you in. After sex, you might have a robust, unassailable feeling, or just as easily a small creeping minuscule feeling. You might have the cardboard feeling of tilting over. Or the gimlet-eyed feeling. Sometimes sex made you giddy and light. It also could make you distracted and confused, as if you were picking up foreign radio frequencies. You might feel tremendous satisfaction and freedom, fortified to stride out into the world and do whatever it was your duty turned out to be. Other times you found your attention funneled down to one narrow track, the opposite of freedom, when your thoughts were only about the lover, about when you'd see him again, about what he was thinking, about when you'd have more of his sweetness.

Sometimes she felt clear and focused and smooth, like a paperweight. Or she was exhausted and flattened.

Sometimes she could not get enough and was unable to stop and her exhausted greedy arms would reach for him again.

Or she'd be satiated utterly, drowsy, full.

She might want to weep uncontrollably.

She might want to laugh.

She might feel at peace with the world, deeply connected to him, and therefore to all humanity. Or want only to crawl off under the nearest rock and die.

She could gaze at a lover sleeping and feel gratitude and adoration. Or fume with frustration. Sometimes even after a lover's tender attentions, she might feel ignored or bereft.

If things lined up she'd feel secure. Or sore. She might be overwhelmed by an urge to embrace everything (the first thing would be him) or a desire simply to sleep. She might want, for a moment, to be left alone. But more often, she wanted to swim up into his arms and stay there forever.

✦

THAT BEAUTIFUL TIME she stood near him in the dark . . . Well, he thought, that's over now.

✦

WHAT DID SHE really want anyway? Could she picture settling down with one man for the rest of her life? It was a nice idea, but were people built that way?

She hadn't been able to stay with her longtime boyfriend, Angus. After six years, when it came time to decide if they were going to get married, she just couldn't do it. She was twenty-eight. Angus loved her; she loved him, but it was in a certain way, not in the *total* way that her instinct (there it was again, that instinct) told her did exist.

Her difficulty envisioning a life with Angus probably had more to do with her own failings, but it *felt* like it was something missing in him. She met Angus in New York after college. He was the friend of her friends Tamara and Gary, who lived down the block (she was living in Brooklyn then, the third of her so far ten apartments) so Angus was around a lot. She probably wouldn't have gotten together with him if they hadn't inadvertently spent so much time together. Her main boyfriend in college had been totally different. Jake was seductive and druggy, and gave her intense, possessive attention when he wasn't giving it to someone else, i.e. sleeping with her roommate. He had such a hold on Kay that she continued to see him, through rehab and even on and off afterward when he'd moved in with an older woman who was supporting him. Angus, in other words, was a hero in comparison with Jake. He paid for dinner and called when he said he would. He was never jealous. He worked as an editor of business pamphlets and was diligent but had quirky taste in shoes and from the start treated Kay as if they would always be together. Initially she liked thinking that way, too. It was a nice idea. But after a few years of domesticity, she found herself looking at Angus with expectation. She waited for him to say something more at the breakfast table. More and more she was waiting for him to turn over to face her in bed. Once, returning from visiting his parents in Pennsylvania, she had the claustrophobic feeling sitting next to him as he drove that the two of them had nothing in common and that her real self was the one at work who blushed when the lighting technicians flirted with her. She knew the value of Angus. He had patience and steadfastness and she used to cling to his long back as if it were a life raft. Their life was tranquil and their bed, one might say, was becalmed. Angus thought she was too concerned with sex.

'You focus on it too much,' he said. 'It's overrated.' They were at an inn in France on vacation, a time Kay felt was rather conducive to sex. Angus wanted to rest. It made it hard for her to picture a future with him. When they were first together, exchanging stories of their sexual past during that limited period when lovers feel free to disclose anything, a period of time which definitely ends, Angus told her about sleeping with the Panamanian maid of a friend of his. He'd met her in the pantry in the middle of the night and they did it on the floor. Kay was thrilled to hear he had it in him. But he must have seen Kay in a different light, and though she waited for it, she never got that sort of treatment from Angus.

Kay used sex as a gauge, despite its paradoxes. She found it easier to read the signals she got from touching someone than to make the more complex discernments of character having to do with responsibility and honor. Those qualities mattered to her, but overshadowing them was the vague but weightier notion of the life force in a person, a person's bigness of heart. A person willing to make contact with other people—that was one of the most appealing things. And people who were struggling. They were appealing, too. Usually the people struggling happened to be messes, but that was because they were taking in more of life. Intact people had ruled a lot of things out. They were less open. It was easy to see the openness in people who were wrecks. And, she had noticed, wrecks were often more likely to give a high priority to sex.

So she'd left Angus. She continued to envision a lifelong situation with another person, just not with someone she actually knew. It was easy to envision it with an unknown person. And children, she figured, would come eventually. She just didn't have the urge yet.

At the moment, sex with Benjamin was putting her in a very receptive state of mind. Was he what she really wanted?

The answer was simple and immediate: yes. An image came to her, of the concentrated look he used to get on the set attempting to answer three questions at once, staring down penetratingly at his sneakers. Yes, she was sure of this. The intensity of her conviction was so strong she felt it must be making her body glow, like something radioactive.

◆

IT WAS a disturbing change, Vanessa keeping him at arm's length. His Vanessa. She became the aloof one, and the aloof person has the power. Vanessa was acting as if she didn't even care she had the power, that's how aloof she was.

But she still was permitting him to see her. They had dates. If it was a Saturday night date, he was pretty much guaranteed to spend the night back in his old bed. One Saturday night she told him, her eyes going a little cross-eyed, which happened when she was being intent, that she was getting serious about this guy she'd been seeing. Some joker who worked with her father. Benjamin didn't eat for a week.

He caught a bad flu. He lay in his basement sublet surrounded by this other guy's knickknacks, delirious, with visions of Vanessa's long legs hooked around another man's back. He called her repeatedly on the phone. Sometimes she'd talk to him nicely and sometimes not. It was Kay all over again.

It was around that time that Patty, the editing assistant with the shiny black hair, came and brought him soup, and they'd had that little thing. And around then was when he asked out Olga who worked at the Cuban place where he had breakfast every morning and suddenly like spring bursting into leaf all these girls started to appear, girls at casting calls, girls he met at parties of people he sort of knew. He was still preoccupied with Vanessa, but a new world of girls was opening up. It was a consolation. There were some very nice girls out there, sweet girls. He didn't stop wanting to be with Vanessa, but thoughts of her pained him and it was a relief to forget her for moments here and there. The moment he stepped out of these girls' beds the thought of Vanessa would return, but he would've had an hour or two, or maybe a night, of not feeling like such a disappointment. He liked seeing these girls who weren't talking about the future or commitments or *working it out* or *working on it*, but instead were opening the shadows at the front of their shirts. They drew close to him. They were smiling and unworried. Each different pair of eyes had a different level of brightness or sadness or sophistication and was always interesting. And all these girls—where had they come from?—seemed to share a total lack of qualms about unbuckling his belt and unbuttoning his pants. It seemed as if every girl was willing to do that. One girl told him she didn't really consider it sex. What Kay was doing to him right now. Another girl said she thought it was intimate, like dancing is intimate. It was something romantic.

He felt these girls *accepted* him. They were sympathetic. They slapped his arm in a frisky way, they rolled their eyes as if to say, Aw you, nothing matters that much, we're all friends here. But best of all, in their faces he saw no signs of hurt he might have caused. After a while, hurt was all he saw on Vanessa's face in the form of a bruised childish expression. He shuddered to think of it. And on Kay's face—well, it had been there practically from the beginning, the tight jaw, her lowered gaze. It seemed the longer you were with a woman the more hurt you put in her expression. He was tired of seeing it. He didn't need to be reminded what an asshole he was.

What might be more helpful to address was his trying to be with just one woman. It's what he wanted eventually, but it was becoming more and more apparent that he would always *like* knowing other women. He couldn't help it; it was biological. Maybe he was incapable of loving only one woman the way she deserved to be loved. The way his mother, for instance, was loved. If that were true, then he should just take himself out of the race. He shouldn't be with anyone. He told each woman he slept with as much. He even sort of meant it.

✦

HER SLAVELIKE posture was arousing to her. She imagined him saying crude things. That aroused her further.

Though he wasn't saying anything. He was silent. He was slumped back against the pillows, his arm still lay to the side. His posture seemed to say, I am only being temporarily detained. In the past, he had conveyed to her how much he liked this, but he did not look overwhelmed.

But then, Kay had never heard a man say he didn't like this. Even the evocation of a blow job would, in conversation, invariably elicit bluster, or a leering look. And yet she'd been with men who grew skittish when she moved down there. There was often more awkwardness than enthusiasm. It could undermine a girl's confidence. It was easy for confidence to be undermined in sex. People got very shy doing this intimate thing, and no one seemed to want to face the fact that sex was complex. They had a hard time talking about it. Lust was simple; it just happened and grew, and if nothing interrupted it, all went smoothly. But personalities were full of interruptions.

People were surprisingly inarticulate on this subject they were supposedly so interested in. That was one of the alluring things about having sex with someone, you got to find out his attitudes. You got to experience a hidden part of that person. It was like getting near the source.

It was rare, the person with a lot of ease in sex. You needed to think for yourself, and not be tangled in preconceptions and misinformation which might have gotten lodged in your psyche way back. It also helped to have a doctor's knowledge of the body, if not a prostitute's.

Kay understood the shyness. She was prey to it, too. Apparently Catholicism could take some blame. But she was working on it. She was trying to pry herself open. She discovered, though, there were certain things you could learn only in bed. Once when she was waitressing, she had a flirtation with a guy she worked with. He had a gruff brutish manner. They ended up in bed one night and everything was going along liquidly and smoothly and she pushed against him and he pushed back and at one point she sort of ground her cheekbone against his cheekbone and he cried out, *Ouch.* And she thought, Oh guess not. You had to get close to find these things out. And even then you learned just a fraction of the whole unexplored vastness of what went on inside a person.

To Kay it seemed impossible to learn a lot of these things about sex if you were with only one person.

That had been one of her attractions to Benjamin. His boldness looked to her like a fresh natural attitude. He just grabbed the girl. That was nice and straightforward.

On one level, at least.

In bed you imagined scenarios. She imagined now she was being forced by him to do this. She was doing what he had ordered her to do. She was eager to please. Though it wasn't always like that. She didn't always feel the same eagerness to obey, the same zest. Sometimes it was distasteful, the exact thing she didn't want to do. Sometimes she'd do it purely for his sake, a treat for him, and sometimes the sweetness of it would miraculously gather in her. She'd met a makeup girl on a job once who said she reached orgasm doing this. Another girl she knew liked doing this better than anything else in sex and had managed to find a boyfriend who didn't like it at all.

Sometimes being far from the person's face, she got a sort of alienated feeling. But at other times, like now, she felt minutely close to him, close to a crucial part of him.

Kay was always surprised when she heard other women (those waitresses had really had some mouths on them) talking about size and prowess and lusting after penises because, really, in and of themselves, how desirable were they as separate entities? It depended a lot on whom they were attached to. The rare glimpse of a penis when she was young—a teenage boy at a pool house, her father coming out of the bathroom and rewrapping his towel—had been fascinating, but not particularly titillating. It was scary. That is, men were. She was right to be scared. Look how much damage men could do. And they didn't even have to know it. They could really ruin a person.

◆

HE LOOKED down at Kay. Hair lying across one cheek, bare shoulder. Her eyes were open a slit and glazed. She looked as if she were on opium.

Kay didn't like drugs particularly. She drank, not a lot, wine usually. When she drank she became more amorous. He'd only seen her what could barely be called drunk a few times. The same could not be said for Benjamin, particularly lately. Fact is, he'd probably done more drugs in the last six months than in the previous six years.

After the broken-down mournful period when he'd moved out of Vanessa's, he began to get his strength back. If nothing else, he was free to do as he pleased. And if that meant imbibing chemicals and giving himself the impression that he was launching on a great adventure, then what was to stop him? There was no Vanessa waiting to get mad that he was out late. He didn't have to think about pacing himself or to hold back having another vodka tonic. He could be himself.

When he first went out with Donald Deitch, it was a challenge to keep up. He couldn't believe a guy could live this way. Donald Deitch hit the town every night. Donald was an actor who'd starred in a surprise low-budget hit five years before and was still best known for that. He'd been in *The Last Journalist* as a favor to Benjamin and they had gotten to be friends. Donald had a girlfriend, Sheryl, who sometimes came out, looking foxy and bored in satin halters, and when she didn't appear, Benjamin wondered what he told her on those nights. Because there were girls everywhere.

He marveled that these girls had been out here all the time. All those years of puzzling over video choices with Vanessa, or reading a book in bed beside her, these girls were all out here. So, O.K., maybe they weren't the women of his life, still, they were nice girls and fun and had a lot of heart. Their lives had been a little rougher, some of them, than those of the daughters of Washington bigwigs or girls who went to private schools in Connecticut, though to be honest he didn't hear that much about the lives of these girls. He didn't hear much about that as they shook back their hair after bending over a mirror and handing along the rolled bill to the next person. They were mischievous and game. Their eyebrows went up, they smiled shyly, they straightened their spines, aware they were being watched. Eventually their glitter-painted fingernails would creep over and rest on his sleeve. They were willing. He didn't need to profess his eternal devotion. Often the girls were trying to seduce *him*.

Maybe this was where he belonged, with these girls. He'd proven himself unsuccessful in being faithful—maybe these girls were the right thing for him. Sure, he missed being attached to Vanessa, but staying with her meant he'd miss out on this whole other aspect of himself. And, sure, he'd like to have a family. One day. If he ever got it together. Though it would probably have to be with a smart but more simple girl. A simple girl, by his description, was one who adored him and would be a good mother to his children and would busy her-self with that. She wouldn't care if, now and then, he went off the beaten track. She could live with it because she knew how men were. She wouldn't want to know about it. She would only ask that it not be thrown in her face, that he not be baldly disrespectful. She'd look the other way. She was smart. She accepted how men were and didn't take it personally. She knew it wasn't anything against her. But most importantly, she loved him. That was the sort of woman he would probably have to find.

But in the meantime these other girls suited him. They recognized his true nature and weren't asking for fidelity and didn't have expectations. Fact is, they hardly asked for any-thing, just to have a good time. They sometimes came up to him at the bar breathlessly asking him if he was partying, or as they walked together out of some club would ask him to drop them off on his way home or even to borrow some cash and if it cost him a little, then, in a way, all the better. When it came down to it, if money changed hands then the exchange was understood and everyone was happy. You got a little action and the girl got some free fun. They were happy, they were sweet girls. They genuinely seemed to like him. He fig-ured it was probably because he was a little different from the types they were used to putting up with. He wasn't really *in* this scene, he was just passing through it. He knew better than to end up like the fifty-year-old geezers chatting up the permed women in tight skirts at the end of the bar at Mary Lou's at 3 a.m. He would never fall that low.

◆

AS KAY grew older, it only became more perplexing, the enormous influence boys had. Kissing, for instance. A girl had to be careful whom she kissed. Just kissing did something. It actually had a chemical effect. It was possible to kiss a person you had a neutral attitude to and a chemical seemed to be released, or something, because the boy whom moments before was not someone you had been regarding longingly could suddenly turn into an object of intense interest or distraction and possible obsession and very likely pain. One of Kay's friends called it boy poison—a boy's kisses were like a poison which infected you and after exposure you craved more, like an addict.

This did not, however, seem to be the case with a boy after he got kissed, or more particularly, after he'd slept with a girl. It was one of the differences between the sexes, that sex, for the most part and very generally speaking, often had the opposite effect. That is, once a boy felt he'd made a conquest, then his energy was *released* and he was free to move on and put the girl out of his mind. For a girl, that conquest left its hook in.

Of course, this didn't always happen. Women were sometimes not susceptible to the boy poison, and mysterious influences were known to make men want to stay. But Kay did not see a lot of that happening close around her. She only saw it from afar. For her, in New York City at the end of the twentieth century, she did not see a lot of roots between men and women fixing themselves in the ground.

Sure, this man had driven her crazy. He was a minefield. Hidden dangers lay in him everywhere. But right now, above the pulled-back bedspread, she'd pushed past the worry of those smaller considerations. If she was adrift, then adrift was the thing she would embrace. She would find the value in adrift. She was taking herself to a higher plain. What could be dangerous in this expansive benevolence? For that's what she felt full of: benevolence and acceptance. Mixed in with physical desire, the moment was only more rich and sweet. It was serene. She was savoring every bit of it. Such a small portion of their history had been serene or benevolent or sweet.

◆

HE WAS DAMNED. He was sure of it.

◆

ANOTHER LITTLE pang of worry swam up through her languid thoughts. It was a small pang. It grew out of the fact that she was lavishing all this adoration on a man who had, frankly, put her through the wringer. He'd lied after he'd vowed not to lie. He gave her little hopes, then yanked them away. Perhaps it would have been better if he'd not given her anything in the first place. But the small disturbance was swallowed up with the softening of her body. She wasn't asking for anything now, and wasn't that the real sign of loving, to give everything out and not ask for anything back?

Out of the corner of her eye she saw a wedge of light reaching the front of the bureau. The sun didn't make it into the room this way in the winter. It lay low on the windowsill. Now, if the curtain was pulled back, sunlight would be flooding one whole side of the room.

◆

THERE WERE ASPECTS of this indulgent life which were not *altogether* detrimental. He was seeing a different side of life. He was learning things—for instance, that he didn't always want to live this way. He'd get back to the projects that he wanted to do, meanwhile he was learning a little more about the business from hanging out with Donald. He and Donald both agreed what a joke Hollywood was. The only reason to deal with Hollywood was for the money and Donald did that, he admitted it, but he wasn't taken in by the game. He lived in New York. He wouldn't *want* the life of one of those Hollywood guys. Benjamin heard the spiel many late nights. For his part, Benjamin felt he'd proven himself, to some degree, with his movie, it had gotten some attention. He'd had an eleven-year relationship, he'd made that effort. So who could begrudge him a little cutting loose? Though even he had to admit, lately it was getting out of hand.

He couldn't remember the last time he'd gone to bed before three. Usually it was more like six. He'd seen the sky lightening into day far more than he'd seen it darkening into night. But living this counterlife bent his thoughts in new directions; it opened up his perspective. Not that he ever saw a sunset in New York anyway. Unless you were high up in a building or happened to glimpse it at the end of one of the big avenues going east-west, all you knew of the sunset was a darkening in the air. No wonder people in New York were so unbalanced. They were totally untouched by the rhythms of nature. You were only aware of nature when something extreme happened, like a snowstorm or a heat wave.

What he really probably ought to do was get out of the city. That's what he needed. Seeing Kay made him realize that. He was nearing the end of a long bender and when it was over he would get out. Away from Donald and temptation. He'd rent some place up near Jeffrey and Andre's house upstate. They'd look after him. They were a good domestic influence with their tag sales and homemade soup, and he could start working on the new script. The only reason he was staying in the city was to hear about whether that music video was going to come through, and then there was the possibility of that low-budget thing if those guys could raise the money, which reminded him, he better give them a call. Before the end of the week, he really should. Shit, was it Thursday already? He definitely better do that tomorrow . . . wait, was Kay saying something? She must be getting tired. At least, a little. But he shouldn't think of that, of her getting tired. When he thought of her, it made him lose, in a weird way, some of his enjoyment. Which was ironic, this being sex. You'd think that if you were having sex with someone, thinking of them would intensify it, but sometimes it was the opposite. Sometimes, if you were concerned, it was best not to think of them at all. Concern wasn't part of the drive. The drive was, ultimately, to *invade* her, overpower her, not protect her. The protective feeling appeared at other times, but not during sex. So much missing was the protective feeling that Benjamin marveled that women actually liked it, which they definitely appeared to at times. They *liked* being penetrated that way. It was when they didn't seem to be enjoying themselves that it made more sense to him. It never ceased to surprise him when they did.

He'd better empty his mind. Everything always moved along more smoothly when there was no real thought going on.

◆

THE INEXPLICABLE thing was, the thing you weren't supposed to like in a person, she liked in him. She was drawn to how wayward he was. She was embarrassed to admit that it had a sexy aspect to it, the shiftlessness with the soulfulness. She was fascinated by the oblivion with which he tilted into women and tried to get under their clothes. Sometimes he seemed unaware of the world around him, then suddenly very keen. She couldn't figure it out. She wasn't scared off by the fact that he wasn't a *smart choice*, she preferred it. His waywardness seemed directly tied to his interest in sex. He wasn't just interested in it, he liked it. Not all men did, contrary to popular lore, not in her experience. Many men purported to be interested in sex, to be *after only one thing* and all that, and then when it came right down to actual contact they didn't really *delight* in it, they could easily be oddly unmoved. It was as if it involved too much interaction. Their attentions were often aloof and rather cool, as if they couldn't quite inhabit them. She'd encountered that a few times. So she appreciated it when a man seemed genuinely interested in women, even if that interest ended up being directed at whatever girl happened to be crossing his path, or sitting beside him at dinner, or bringing him his cup of coffee. Along with Benjamin's disorganization and democratic taste in women was a lack of having formulated strong ideas about how a woman ought to be or about trying to get her to act in a certain way. He had a lack of expectation that a woman be demure or obedient or fun or whatever it was a man supposedly wanted a woman to be. Benjamin just seemed to like how women *were*. She liked that open, lax attitude. It allowed her to be how she was. It allowed her to be free.

Of course, those wayward qualities which in the beginning were appreciated and inspiring soon became the very things which made her suffer.

◆

THEY NEVER REALLY did have a chance, he thought. He and Kay had started out on the wrong foot and how can it ever be right if you start out with so many things out of order. They didn't have a prayer.

It was hard to look at her now. He didn't want to look at her with pity. Suddenly he thought of that time in Mexico when she climbed over the cement wall with the jagged top. He'd held her bare foot in his clasped hands. She'd thrown her sandals over the wall and he was giving her a leg up and she placed her foot in his hands. Her leg was braced against his shoulder after she stepped up and he tried to hold her steady. Mesmerized, he watched her swing the other leg firmly up. He wobbled a little, keeping ahold of her foot, then she stepped out of his hand, relieving him of her weight, and even then he knew they didn't have a prayer.

◆

BUBBLES OF DOUBT popped to the surface of her certainty. But wasn't it more real, to have doubt? Shouldn't you expect a little doubt in everything?

The last night in Mexico, after the last day of filming, they sat in the far corner of the hotel bar. They were returning the next day to New York. He looked miserable which she had appreciated. His face was fixed in a stricken, doglike expression. He stared at her, unable to speak. They ordered a late dinner and hardly ate the food and took the elevator up to his floor. They walked solemnly close to each other down the hallway to his door. Inside, a muffled phone was ringing. He slipped the white card into the key slot and the door clicked open to blackness and a loud ringing. He winced, half facing her. 'Go on,' she said. He checked her face to see if she meant it, and went forward hunched into the gloom. She waited at the doorway. He glanced back over his shoulder, a pale mournful face giving her one last look out of the shadows, then he picked up the receiver.

'Honey!' he said.

He threw back his head and jauntily shot out his leg, locking the knee. His posture lifted up. His voice was breezy and happy and genuine. Kay's blood ran cold. She felt as if she were watching the first few sparks spit from a cracked pipe in an unattended corner of a factory just before the whole plant explodes.

Why didn't she shut the door there and then? She was frozen. She was shocked. She was hurt. But some damaged part of her stirred. Some damaged thing in her was invigorated. One could almost say she liked it, the slam of emotion. It went directly to her heart. Maybe it came out of her heart.

His complete and utter disregard for her had a transforming effect. It made her disappear. She no longer stood in the door. She was ignored out of existence. He'd had the power to do that. The slamming feeling, even if it was painful, was better than no feeling at all.

Afterward, her practical, protective nature prevailed and she removed herself from him. Then her weaker nature crept forth, entertaining unrealistic expectations, and she gave him little slivered chances. Neither had worked. And now? Now came her wide, openhearted nature, her letting-go nature, her what-will-be-will-be nature, her not-judging-another-person nature. It was fueled by goodness and acceptance and love.

Those bubbles of doubt were minuscule in this vast ocean. Why worry about some unaccountable things? Particularly things you could do nothing about. One must let go of all that and simply surrender.

And there was this lovely feeling to surrender to. She sank into a soft pad where logistics and personal foibles and pre-conceptions melted down to small lumps. She saw Benjamin simply as a man, someone with the power to overwhelm her. If she was lucky he would break her and demean her into oblivion. Her mouth was around him and her hand held him down and inside her a pleasant chaos whirled. In the whirling she felt savage and depraved.

◆

HIS MIND unmonitored roamed. Kay shifted and started to do something with a slightly different grip. He tried to stay with it, but he kept flashing on the other recent administrations he'd been getting in those dim rooms with girls in shiny tops and their high heels pigeon-toed behind them. They were kneeling before him, with that shadow at their breasts. He reached out to part the shirt. The girls pushed him onto his back. There'd been one who slipped under the restaurant table and undid his pants with everyone there. There was that girl named Zizi who wanted him to bite her, the Peruvian movie star with a fired-up look even more wasted than he was. Parts of the nights were blurred, other moments were clear as freeze-frames. In the mornings he woke with his clothes on, frail as an eggshell, unsure of his journey home. The afternoon light appeared behind the diamond grid on his window and he would think how strange it was that he had once moved around in daylight.

It was even surreal in Kay's room now, in the late afternoon with the bright yellow band of light on the long side of the curtain. He'd sort of forgotten that people did things like made tomato sandwiches for lunch and kept flowers on the windowsill. He was not high now, and his body felt the difference. It was not necessarily a better feeling. At the moment what he felt most was weary. Too weary to move. Everything was addled. Images from his nights were worming their way into this room. It was hard to believe he'd gotten a thrill being let into the back entrance of some place with Donald. At this point he would have welcomed Vanessa's *Where were you?* expression. He remembered a girl one night in a white dress. She wasn't carrying a bag or anything so she looked unfettered and superior. The girl wouldn't let him buy her a drink. She barely glanced at him. She didn't want to have anything to do with him. It had bothered him. He usually could get a girl's attention. So he ended up with another girl wafting with perfume in a backseat with Donald on the other side of her . . . no, he didn't want to think of that. He looked at Kay. Through a part in her hair a small earring trembled. It was silver, shaped like an egg.

He reached down for her shoulder and tried to bring her up to him. Maybe if they were closer. Maybe if he saw her face, or if he was kissing her, he'd feel more *engaged*. But, no, she was shaking her head. She wanted this. He didn't have the strength to try to persuade her, he didn't have the conviction. She was intent. Let her then. He closed his eyes.

They sort of lurched toward him, these body parts of other women, their breasts, their lips, their unzipped skirts. From his position in Kay's bed they weren't looking so enticing. From this point of view they were losing their luster. He mustn't think about that. It occurred to him that if he looked at it too long, a pain would start. It would hurt. He tried sweeping his mind clear. Sky. He thought of sky.

There was a golf ball sailing through the sky. It flew up from a good, squared-off stroke. He saw the fifth hole of the golf course on Fishers Island where he'd been once. It was a rosy evening. That was better. A man walked in the distance. He bent down to right a ball. A swallow swooped overhead. Then he was driving on a highway in an open car, the green signs were gliding by tilting down. He passed a sea wall. There was Monica Vitti in *L'Avventura* walking along it, her heels clicking on the pavement, wearing a narrow black skirt.

His thoughts wavered for a moment and he had a flash of

some girl from the other night or the other week. She was standing in front of a blue wall, bending down to pick up her bag. Her skirt came up and the lamplight shone on the back of her thigh and on a green bruise. Then there was the coffee table at Donald's apartment: the white-streaked mirror next to the stack of car magazines, the green glass blob of an ashtray full of butts. His mood dipped. He forced his mind to swerve in a better direction, upward.

He was carrying a flag up a hill. It was windy, the flag flapped with a noble sound. He could see rooftops spreading far away and the sea in the distance. He swooped down to one old building with stairs on the outside and a woman in bare feet waiting at the door. He thought of a clip from an old Ed Wood movie, of a man clutching his head with both hands and grimacing. A radio was knocked off a table. Then it was back on the table, an old radio with yellow shellacked siding and brown dials. Scratchy static, then dance music. A farmhouse set on a wide prairie. There was a farmer on a tractor, bumping slightly up and down. A flock of birds took off behind the farmer, startled by gunshot. A woman stepped out the door of the farmhouse onto the porch, rubbing sweat from her neck. Out of the woods came a row of soldiers holding up a row of shotguns. They looked up: a fan of fighter jets sliced the sky in formation, in the shape of a stingray. Then he was in his fourth-grade classroom with the flesh-colored desks. An eraser bounced off the blackboard, leaving a white corner. He thought of the girls going into the girls' bathroom, of the girls' knees above their kneesocks and their short skirts. He thought of the abandoned house behind the playing fields where they sometimes snuck at recess. He hadn't thought of that in years. It had a cement floor and the brown leaves were scratchy and dry on it. You always tried to catch a glimpse of the girls' underwear. It wasn't hard. Kay made a low noise. He thought of Kay walking in front of him, on a path in the woods, wearing her black dress with the hem fluttering. He watched her from behind. Yes, that was doing something. He was getting closer. Was she gripping harder or was that him getting bigger? A moving mass of hats flooded by, men on their way to work in the morning, charging through Grand Central Station. It was another time in history, a time he'd never seen, a time he'd never even known. Yes, he was getting there.

✦

IT WAS COMING together now and that's all that she could count on.

She knew, way in the back of her mind, that there was a trapdoor somewhere. There was always a trapdoor. But by definition, the trapdoor was where you didn't expect it, so why waste time trying to position yourself to avoid it? She would try to stay with this transcending feeling for as long as she could.

And at the moment she was feeling what surely must be the best feeling there was. Rapture.

She was creeping slowly to the center of herself. He was the bridge she took to get there. Around her was a steep universe, dark at the edges, encroaching. There were rocks with inky shadows and tree branches against a night sky. Did he know how he was carrying her? Could he feel it?

She felt as if a powerful magnet were pulling her up against resisting air. Her body kept meeting waves of pressure and pressing through them. Everything was swimming upward. She rode the steep rises and something luminous and thin ran up and down her spine. Light was coming out of— out of her ears, out of her forehead! She was radiating light. Stiff wings beat in her head. Her mouth was battered. Everything around her was lifted and golden and electric.

✦

HE THOUGHT OF the fact that Kay was here with him and how he never thought that would happen again. And after today he was certain it never would. As soon as she found out he was going straight from her to Vanessa, that would do it. She might not find out now, but she would, eventually.

He'd completely lost track of the time and it was very possible that he was late and that Vanessa was already starting to wait. Though even her waiting had changed. It wasn't as firm as before. She didn't have as much invested in it. Even that was probably temporary. It wasn't hard for him to imagine her ceasing altogether to wait for him. He could see it. Some things he could see clearly, even in the haze his life had become. He saw that the hands he'd been holding recently and the breasts he'd leaned on and the mouths he'd been kissing were not the hands or breasts or mouths of a person he loved.

The other night he was coming home in a cab. It was before dawn but the sky had started to get light. The sun hadn't hit any of the buildings and the city still looked muted and gray. He was slumped back with his head on the seat, burnt out. His cab stopped at a cross street and an Asian guy on a bicycle pedaled past. The guy was balancing a big round bag just below his handlebars. His posture was upright and erect. He wasn't a young man and he had an industrious air: up before sunrise, pedaling to work. On top of his helmet was a blinking red light, a square ruby. The guy was really looking out for himself, Benjamin thought. The helmet was one level of protection, the blinking light an extra one. Benjamin figured he probably had a wife at home, and kids, so he was worth being looked after. Seeing the guy made Benjamin feel pretty lousy. He didn't actually *want* to be that guy, but he still felt like a loser.

He felt short-circuited, like some crude science experiment, wired by kids in a garage. The tenderness he had for Kay, he knew it was somewhere in him, but it had slipped off. He often had a recurring dream of being on the wing of an airplane which was tipping and by some miracle he would manage, by flattening himself to the wing, not to slip off. It defied the laws of physics, but he stayed on. It was like that with Kay: it defied laws. There was no reason he should be staying on.

He tried fleetingly to find that tenderness for her. He waded through the scenes of being pushed back and being sucked and stroked by god knows who god knows where. He saw Kay on the beach in Mexico with the whites of her eyes showing up in the dimming light. Then she zoomed off as if shot by a cannon and he was standing at the yawning edge of a great brown pit under a stony sky. Across the canyon he saw a puny little stick figure on the opposite side. It was Kay. Not waving. Just looking at him.

He tried to sink into base sensation. He heard his breathing. He saw a barren landscape, like something on the moon, except damp. He concentrated on the solitary figure looking at him. He was breathing harder.

♦

HER FACE flushed deeply.

She wished that he could be feeling this, she hoped she was amazing him. The room suddenly went lighter and the walls were white and soft. His skin was soft and he'd gotten just now even harder.

Out of the smoke of battle he seemed to appear to her, disoriented, in tatters, returning. She would welcome him. She'd take him in. A wave of gratitude swept through her and she had a terrible urgency to hold on to him, to keep him here. The desire gripped her feverishly, like a sickness. She wanted to hold fast to the beauty of him and to the feeling of love and to the notion that at some point in the past they'd loved each other and that she'd known how it felt to be loved by him and that she loved him now and even if nothing came after this, she would have at least the resolution of this afternoon. Their being together would stay here in the room and be a thing she could look in on through the half-closed door when she wanted. She would see herself lying alongside him and be able to conjure up the feeling of union that went along with it. She would always have it to see. It would never disappear, not till she carried it off with her when she died. A thought flickered through the spots in front of her eyes: there must have been other times like this she'd already forgotten. When had they been?

One could hold on to only so many memories at once. A big memory required a lot of attention to keep it alive. You had to visit it often, or the memory would fade. Maybe this memory was replacing another memory no longer being checked on. Well, that was bound to happen.

Above her she could hear him breathing more quickly. More shallowly. Then in his throat she heard a low groan.

The sound sent a flare through her. Her heart was racing so fast she felt she might black out. Her head vibrated and her hand and eyes were clenched tight and she heard his long intake of breath sort of shuddering. Then he was silent and her mouth felt the small spasm. He released his breath in a long sigh and she felt the liquid in her mouth full, neither warm nor cool, but the same temperature as her mouth, the exact same temperature as herself.

◆

IT SLIPPED OUT of him weakly. It seemed to spill out on its own, before he even had a chance to register it. It sort of came out before he meant it to, without any fanfare, happening without his say-so.

◆

SHE HAD a surreal two-dimensional feeling, suddenly still. She felt like a cutout, hovering over his body, hovering just off the bed. She thought oddly of the moment in church when you cross yourself and how curious it was you could bless yourself and not need someone else to do it and she kept ahold of him with her lips soft now and her hand slack, but still in position. They were both quiet. She tasted him, pale gray, pooling in her mouth. It didn't make sense, but it seemed to taste numb.

Her heart, which had been bursting, now slowed down and everything was still.

The liquid settled in her mouth and she found that in addition to tasting numb, it also seemed to taste slightly forlorn, as if it were aware somehow of having been delivered to a warm wet place, but not the right one.

◆

HE FELT as if he'd emptied out everything good left in him. Then he wondered if, in fact, there had been anything good left.

Goodness was something way back there. He'd crossed the bridge away from it long ago. The moment he stepped off the bridge, up it went in flames. He could still hear the wood spitting and the planks popping. It had all burst into fire when he'd not been able to change his life for a person he loved.

Her head was resting on his upper leg which had fallen dead asleep up to the hip. He pushed the hair back from her temple and she blinked her eyes slowly, catlike. She murmured something. He couldn't hear what. He didn't want to disturb her dreamy mood by asking her to repeat it. At this point there wasn't anything he could imagine hearing that would make much difference anyway. He wished he felt as satisfied as she looked there, collapsed. She lifted her head with a wobbling effort. He saw her throat smooth out when she swallowed. She set her head back down. It was hard to say if her unblinking stare reflected bliss or the blankness you see in the traumatized.

He had a sudden sinking feeling. Something left him: the potential to do anything good again.

Then came a further sinking feeling, lower than all the other ones before it. A sharp little truth hunched there. Whatever goodness he thought he might have had was turning out to be less than he might have hoped.

◆

SHE FELT HIS hand stroking her hair. A need stirred in her, to say something, to tell him what this meant. She wanted him to know, and to tell him everything. What came out sounded much milder than she'd supposed, seeming so intense inside.

"That was worship," she said.

She turned her face up to him and swallowed. Then she lay her head back down. The words shook her. She felt altered in some big nameless way. She stared, not focusing on anything, stunned.

◆

HE WENT to the Grand Canyon once. It was after college, driving out West on his own. He walked the steep paths down into the canyon and spent three days by himself, wandering around. He saw hardly any other people. One morning he woke and opened his small tent flap to all the cliffs and bluffs and ground which when he'd gone to sleep had been red and brown to now being covered in snow. It was like God was down there. When he climbed back up he brought that feeling with him, of there being a force behind everything, a big power. It was something he would always have, he thought, to fall back on.

But he'd lost that feeling now. He couldn't for the life of him recall it.

Here he was in a glowing bedroom which all of a sudden seemed lit up like some flower with the sun flooding the wall, with a woman whom he'd not exactly honored who was, for some reason beyond him, treating him lovingly. He couldn't for the life of him imagine why she was doing that. He couldn't for the life of him imagine that feeling he'd had of belief after being in the Grand Canyon. It was like trying to move your hand through space without muscles to grasp anything.

He shut his eyes. He saw the empty landscape. He knew he had to get out of bed and get going and soon, but he was mesmerized by this vision of emptiness. It was telling him something. The air above the pit began to move. All his sorrow and pain seemed to gather there. It began to swirl around and, whirlpool-like, to pick up force, attracting all the misery and grief in the whole world. The weight of it was being sucked down into the pit.

It was fucking sad. He wondered if Kay had any idea how really fucking sad this was, or how wretched he felt, or how polluted he was, or really how bad. He'd been sliding along in the shadows for a long time so no one could get a really good look at him. Because if they did, they'd see what a truly hideous human being he was.

Well, people found these things out in good time. And she'd learn, soon enough.

Susan Minot was born in Boston, Massachusetts, and grew up in Manchester-by-the-Sea. Her first novel, *Monkeys*, was published in a dozen countries and received the Prix Femina Étranger in France. She is the author of *Evening, Lust & Other Stories* and *Folly*, and she wrote the screenplay for Bernardo Bertolucci's *Stealing Beauty*.

A NOTE ON THE TYPE

The text of this book was set in Centaur, the only typeface designed by Bruce Rogers (1870–1957), the well-known American book designer. A celebrated penman, Rogers based his design on the roman face cut by Nicolas Jenson in 1470 for his Eusebius. Jenson's roman surpassed all of its forerunners and even today, in modern recuttings, remains one of the most popular and attractive of all typefaces. The italic used to accompany Centaur is Arrighi, designed by another American, Frederic Warde, and based on the chancery face used by Lodovico degli Arrighi in 1524.

Composed by Stratford Publishing Services,
Brattleboro, Vermont

Printed and bound by Beryville Graphics,
Berryville, Virginia

Designed by
Dorothy S. Baker